Critical acclaim

"Gripping . . . The combination of dramatic action, romantic interest, and vivid storytelling will grab even the most apolitical teens." (boxed review) —ALA *Booklist*

"Lyrical . . . no background knowledge is needed to become caught up in the drama of the many in this embattled land as related through the eyes of two compelling characters. An excellent first effort." (starred review)
—*School Library Journal*

"Arresting . . . a powerful fictional portrait of the poverty and oppression in contemporary Haiti." (starred review)
—*Publishers Weekly*

"Temple handles, with unobtrusive ease, the intricacies of changing and emerging viewpoints, the juxtaposition of past and present, the blend of political and personal, the balance of romance and violence." (starred review)
—*Bulletin of the Center for Children's Books*

"A deeply felt, provocative statement of human courage by an exciting new author." (starred review)
—*The Horn Book*

TASTE OF SALT
A Story of Modern Haiti

———

FRANCES TEMPLE

HarperTrophy
A Division of HarperCollinsPublishers

Thanks to FATHER FRANTZ GRANDOIT for the title of this book, which he first used for a reading program in Haiti.

Thanks to PRESIDENT JEAN-BERTRAND ARISTIDE, whose sermons and speeches are quoted in this book from his *In the Parish of the Poor: Writings from Haiti*, translated and edited by Amy Wilentz, published by Orbis Books, Maryknoll, New York, copyright © 1990 by Orbis Books. Used with permission.

Thanks also to AMY WILENTZ, whose reporting from Haiti over the years informed much of this story, especially for her book *The Rainy Season: Haiti Since Duvalier* published by Simon & Schuster in 1990.

To the people in
Haiti and the Dominican Republic
whose true and ongoing stories
are woven into this story,
honor, respect, and *bon kouraj*.

CONTENTS

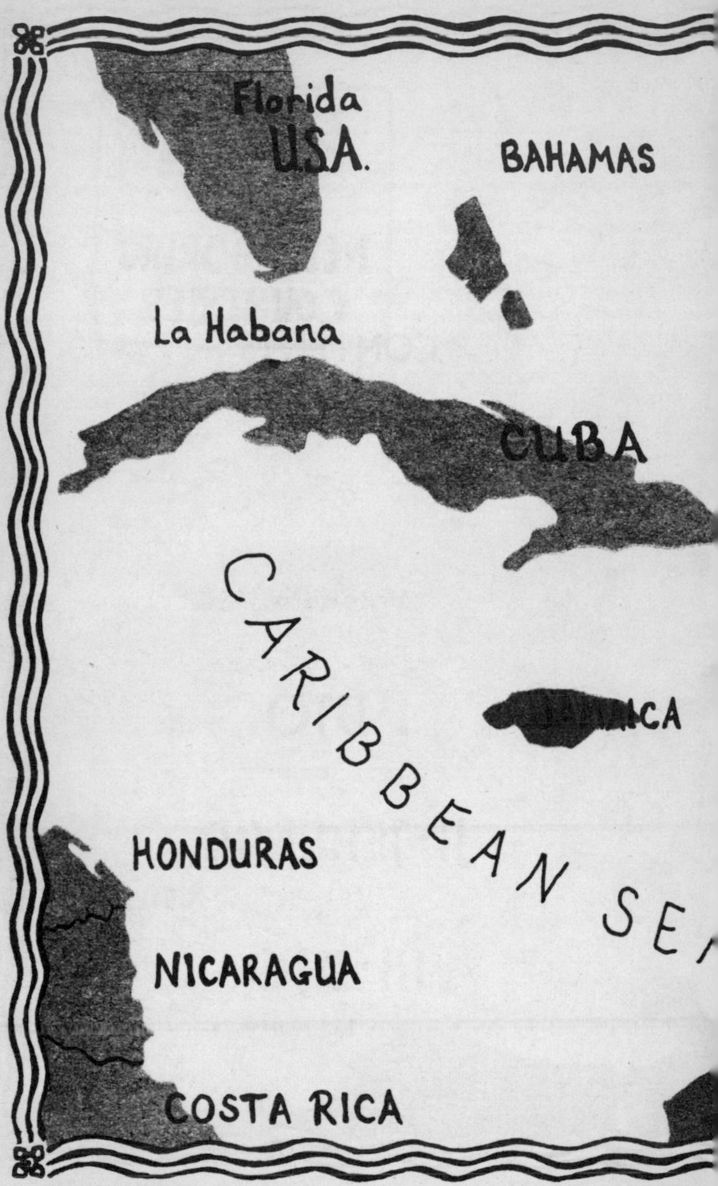
Florida
U.S.A.
BAHAMAS
La Habana
CUBA
CARIBBEAN SE
HONDURAS
NICARAGUA
COSTA RICA

ATLANTIC

┌─────────────────────┐
│ **HAITI**   │
│ **AND**   │
│ **NEIGHBORING**   │
│ **COUNTRIES**   │
└─────────────────────┘

ATLANTIC OCEAN

HAITI DOMINICAN REPUBLIC

Santo Domingo

Port-au-Prince

PUERTO RICO

VENEZUELA

PORT-AU-PRINCE, HAITI
February 1991

I · DJO

1

It is not quiet, here in this make-do hospital, but it is peaceful. A white curtain separates me from the other people who lie here, groaning sometimes, coughing. A window at my feet faces out to the street. I can hear the *taptap* callers, the fresco vendors, the egg seller's shout, the truck horns. But nobody is calling me.

In the soft, warm air floats the flat smell of blood, the sharp smell of pee, the floor bleach. These smells make my eyes water and bring a taste of metal to my throat. They are better than no smells, I think.

I wonder if I will die here.

I watch the white curtain move softly in the breeze. Beside the curtain, someone has written on the wall. NOU RENMEN DJO, it says. KANPE DJO.

We love Djo. Stand up, Djo.

I remember that I am Djo.

Who wrote that? Maybe some small boy from La-fanmi. Lafanmi Selavi, the shelter set up by Father Aristide, the man we call Titid, who also started this clinic. The shelter where I used to live.

Thank you, whoever wrote on the wall. *Chapo ba*: I take my hat off to you.

But don't ask me to get up, little brother. My feet at the bottom of the bed don't take orders from me.

Titid says I can no longer be his bodyguard, since my own body is so broken. Until it is fit again, I can no longer be useful in that way. But Titid says that it is not only the body, with its feet and hands and strong back that can be useful. He says the mind and spirit are useful, too. That mine are still strong, despite the blows. Titid says that for this work of storytelling, I am fit. I don't know if he sees true. What I am is tired. Bright day passes outside the window of this place like a small gold dream. So fast it will be nighttime.

Titid has invited someone to my bedside to listen to my story. He says each time I sleep, I will remember, and when I wake, I must tell everything to the man that brings the tape recorder.

I think Titid is afraid I will die altogether, like Lally,

like Marcel. And if I tell my story to the tape recorder man, whoever he be, then I will not die entirely. Titid loves me. Also Titid is a politician. He knows how to use stories to make things happen, to make the way of the world change. And I am Titid's helper, one of his boys. I did not help him enough, the night the *Macoutes* came and firebombed the shelter. But lying on this cot like some flipped-over cricket, I am still one of Titid's team.

"Ah! Today we are lucky!"

"God smiles. . . ."

"*Komon ou yé?*"

"*Pa pyu mal, mamzelle, pa pyu mal.*"

I hear approving voices up and down the ward. By the commotion, I know that a good-looking woman is coming this way.

And I hear a woman murmur polite old-fashioned greetings in a soft voice:

"Honor. . . . Respect. . . . Honor."

Oh, no. She is coming here, to my end of the hall! Titid has tricked me! It is a beautiful black girl that brings the tape recorder, and here I lie, flat on my backside in this bed, so ugly, so weak. My hair, what was not burned off, is shaved. My head is lumpy from the *Macoutes*' bludgeons. My eyes are swollen half-shut like an old drunkard. I seem one hundred and not seventeen.

And Titid thinks that it is to this woman I will tell my troubles?

What can I do?

No way to hide.

I pretend sleep.

My head hurts. My throat is too dry. I wish suddenly that I can be one or the other: truly alive or else truly dead.

When I open my eyes again, the light from the window is bright. Against it I see the girl, still here. She is biting her fingernails. She is nervous. She is maybe going to cry. Oh, Lord.

"*Mamzelle*." What else can I call her?

The girl jumps a mile. Dead man speak.

"Oh! Excuse. You are Djo?"

I see she has been reading the wall.

"What be left of him," I say.

No smile. "You can talk, Djo?" she asks.

I nod. I can talk, but is a lot of trouble.

"Would you like some water?"

"*Souplé*, please."

She lifts my head to give me water. Very serious and careful. She not touch me at all, only hold the pillow. I think this girl make a good nurse. Then I notice she is shaking.

"Father Aristide gave me this tape recorder machine," she says.

"So he tell me. For my story." Is easier to talk now I have water.

"Do you want to, Djo? Do you want to talk for the tape?" She tries to look at me and quickly turns away. Tears come to her eyes, because she is looking at my own eyes, swollen and bloody.

"You going to splash the water," I tell her.

She sets down the cup, sure enough splashing water. She puts her hands together between her knees. Her knees shaking, even.

This girl is too nervous.

"I will tell you everything if you will tell me your name," I say, to cheer her. She looks at me from the corner of her eye, and she smiles, a little uncertain.

"Jeremie," she says. I think it a beautiful name, like a town I heard of once, with pink and blue houses, by the sea. A funny name for a girl.

"Punch you recorder, then, Jeremie," I say.

If I close my eyes, maybe the girl relax. If I just forget her and make my mind float . . .

"It begins way back," I say. "Back when my mama borned me. In that place in Cité Soleil with the blue walls and the picture of Christ with his red heart, and the green beads that hang in the doorway to keep away flies. This room, our room, is more tall than wide.

"Blue walls, it have. And a red ceiling. First thing I

9

remember is the picture of Jesus. It moves. It flies gently up-down-up-down. At the same time I feel my mama's hand: gently it goes *pat*-pat-pat, *pat*-pat-pat, *pat*-pat-pat on my back. And I smell my mama's neck. She is rocking me in her rocking chair.

"This chair have a creak, like frog song. Is my mama's own. My father gave it to her as marriage present. The chair, with the two beds and the people, fills up the room. Before we came to live here, before my father painted it so fine, this room was a stall for a motorcar. That is why it has no window, my mama explains, and why it is so small and tall.

"And this pretty room full of people: my mama and my sisters Eulalie and Emmeline, my brothers Pie and Lachaud, and my cousin Lally. All we children sleep in one bed, but my mama and father have their own bed, with curtain. The curtain has big yellow check and birds painted on. . . ."

"I know the kind," the girl say. I open my eye a crack and see her smile. There be many such sheets on the lines of Cité Soleil—yellow, pink, and blue.

"In daytime my mama pulls back the curtain so that we children can play on her bed. If first we brush off our feet. . . ."

I see the girl listening, and I begin to watch this girl, and I forget what I was talking about.

"Make it play, Jeremie, to see if that machine works," I say after a while.

So Jeremie listens, and I listen, and my mind floats again from Jeremie to that room in Cité Soleil, Port-

10

au-Prince, Haiti. And I see my daddy, up close. I am sitting on his bony knee, and he is such a fine big black man, with white teeth and a scar on his face. He is looking at the picture of Jesus, and suddenly I ask him, "Why do that man look so sick, with his eyes rolled back like he go into a fit?"

My daddy answers me seriously.

"Djo," he says. "In the picture Jesus just going into a trance. It is because he is the Go-between, going between the true spirit and the human beings like we-all. Beyond him, behind the picture, be spirit. Beyond him be Damballah. . . ."

"And who Damballah, then?" I ask. My daddy looks at my mama. My mama nods her head.

"Spirit of life," says my daddy slowly. "Damballah is god in Guinée Africa and here in Haiti, too."

Then my mama stretches her arms out wide and curves her hands down.

"Like rainbow over all we spirit," she says. Her arms stretch across our whole room.

"What did you say? What is this white place with the sharp smell?"

"It is Titid's clinic, Djo. You are here because the *Macoutes* firebombed the shelter at Lafanmi and beat you up."

She says it gently, her face looking away. I remember her now, the girl with the name like a town.

"I'm sorry, girl. Jeremie. I did drift away."

2

All night I been waiting in the darkness. On one side and another, across the town, I hear roosters. Every hour the roosters think it be morning. They crow so mournful, so hopeful, they wake the dogs. The dogs bark: sometimes they have contest to see who can bark fiercest, and then they try out how they all sound together. The dogs tire. The dogs settle. Then some rooster see a car light and think it sunrise. Begin the whole show again.

To pass the time, I think what I will tell the girl Jeremie.

Now the *taptap* drivers start calling for early passengers: "Jac-mel! Jac-mel!" So I know it will soon be light for true.

Is only when it gets light I can sleep at last, without the dream of smoke and fire and boys screaming.

12

Without the feeling I got to do something quick but I not able to move.

Is day now, full day, because Jeremie is here. She has on a light blue uniform with white blouse. Is a school uniform, from the nuns' school.

This Jeremie, I think she is a baby, really. All she needing be a big bow in her hair. And prickly, too. Scared of me. Is it because I am so ugly now? She sits by the bed on the edge of the chair, like she prepared to run away at any time. If she feel like that, I don't want to talk to her.

"How do you feel today, Djo?" Her voice is more like doctor than friend. But I answer, just because it has been one long night.

"I glad is day." She never know how glad.

"I'm glad, too, Djo," she says.

She touches my hand, just quick. I get shock like electric power.

Then we both quiet like we lose breath. She mess with her recorder machine.

"Where we were, Jeremie?"

"Inside the room where you were born, Djo."

Her eyes water, but she look at me direct today.

"I punch again?" she ask.

"Punch, girl."

My mama smell like garlic clove. For some time, while I am crawling about, she has rocking-chair work. She peels garlic for a restaurant. She works in the middle of us: feet flat on the floor, she leans forward in her chair, takes our green plastic tub full of fresh garlic on her lap, breaks up all the cloves. One by one, she puts the peel in her skirt, and the peeled clove she puts in a red bowl on the floor. When she's tired, she rocks to ease her back. We like the smell, and the sound of her humming. Then one day she full of fury: the man Mama sells her garlic to has lost his job, so Mama has got no market for her garlic. She goes to stripping palm, and cusses when it cuts her hands.

My daddy is not home much, but when he does come home everything is one wonderful *bamboche*: fine nights full of guitar and radio, the smell of fry food, the fire swallow of *clairin*. I ride on my daddy's shoulders, dancing high in the night, with my feet tucked back under my father's arms, holding to his shoulder blades. He starts out holding me, but then he forgets I even there. His dance spreads to his arms, he lets go of my feet, but I hang on, my toes flat against his back. I move my arms like him and feel the drum coming through his muscle and bone, right out through my fingers, high up there in the night.

Two, three days of *bamboche*, then he is gone again. He sends money. Mama keeps the money in a paper in the front of her dress. She loves my daddy, and the money is from him.

Our place has a half door to the street. Mama says let we stay safe inside until we are big enough to climb out. So all the time I am trying to pull myself out.

My best friend from always is my cousin Lally. We play together on my mama's bed, and later I get strong enough to pull up on the door ledge, and I pull Lally up, too.

Lally is a little fellow but very sharp. Is Lally show me how to make boats from orange peel and sail them down the gutter in Rue Michel, how to catch lizard without him leave his tail. Is Lally that learns Mamzelle Louanne has cashews in her tree for to pelt down, or that Ton Jac will beat you with his switch broom if you greet him before noon.

Like my mama says, we children get big mouths. The money Mama makes is not enough to feed us all. Lally and I be sent to find food. Even to search in trash. But ours are not the only hungry bellies in Port-au-Prince, not even the most hungry. If there be any good throwaway, somebody always finds it before me and Lally. . . .

I been dreaming how me and Lally find a fish down by the sea. The fish they pull from water by La Saline give people the bellyache, you know. But since this fish still alive, me and Lally discussing whether to take him home or throw him back. The dream change,

15

and I be the fish. I am looking up at the two boys with my one eye. Waiting for decision.

Somebody missing. This whole hallway Titid uses for a hospital is quiet today. Where is the girl?

I hear feet coming fast up the steps.

"Mornin', Djo! Sister kept me late in school, fixing things for Lent. I ran all the way!"

She puts her schoolbag against the wall and stands by the bed. She is breathing hard, her breast move, her skin glow. She has sweat up close to her hair. I know she don't want to sit down.

"What can I get for you, Djo?"

I want my body back. I going to explode with wanting.

No sound comes out when I try to speak.

The girl hovers like a moth, near, far. She touches my foot, which is sticking out down where I can't see it.

"Got any feeling in your foot, Djo?"

I am angry that people treat my body like it not be my own, like it some monster show.

Jeremie just touch my foot and is as if somebody drag a piece of wood across. I feel sick. But even sick be better than nothing at all.

"Do that some more, Jeremie, very light. I think I do feel it."

16

"They will come back, Djo," says Jeremie, sitting down now. "Your feet going to come back. And . . . everything, too."

"The sisters hand me trouble today, Djo," she says, frowning for a second. Is like a different person suddenly. Tough, moody girl. Then she put back on her smooth face. This Jeremie got layers like onion.

"What kind of trouble they hand you?"

She doesn't answer. "Did you ever go to school, Djo?"

I almost went to school.

One day, Jeremie, a lady comes down Rue Michel. She is looking at children to see which ones be school-age now. Every small child she sees, she says to him, "Put your arm up over your head and grab your ear on the far side." If the child can understand her instruction and can reach his ear so, the child be ready for school. Lally and me, we can reach fine, and we run ahead to teach all the street so they can be ready.

But there is some question of school fee, so Mama says, "Let your sister be teacher for you boys."

My sister Eulalie was two years at the nuns' school when our father had work here in the city.

"If these boys make trouble for you, Eulalie, I my-self go help with the whipping!" says our mama, a gleam in her eye, waving palm. Me and Lally hide

17

from Mama and Eulalie much of the time. What we like is to search in the street for bits of newspaper with stories on them. We keep them in a tin. Our portfolio, Lally calling it.

"Djo! Lally! Where you boys disappearing to so fast?"

"Be portfolio time, Mama!"

"Must work on our portfolio, Tantie!"

With Eulalie's help we do learn letters and numbers. This was my school. I missed only the uniform. And I would not look so fine as you in the uniform, Jeremie.

Two of my teeth are broken off, jagged to touch with my tongue. I am so stupid to try to smile, to forget and act like I a fine-looking fellow again. Not to cry, I shut my eyes and pretend sleep. After a while I peek out, and there is Jeremie, still sitting patiently.

"Are you there, Djo?" she asks. "Do you want to tell me more about Rue Michel and all that? Or do you want to sleep?"

"Both," I say, too sleepy to say more. Mostly I want to sleep and think about Lally.

"This afternoon you tell me the rest, Djo. Sleep now."

Jeremie stands and swings her book bag up over her shoulder. She leans down and puts her hand on mine.

18

"Sleep, Djo," she says. "Dream good dreams. I will come back this afternoon."

I wish I could walk away like that.

Soon Mama decides we are big enough to do serious work. By this I know she means feed ourselves, though we all do share. Mama finds us one old shoe-shine kit, so we can earn money polishing people's shoes.

"You are good drummer already, Djo," she says. "Drum so on the box, and the customers will come running."

She is as excited as me. I drum. She dances. Is going to be a good business. We make the polish out of anything we can find, like old pig grease and palm smear.

The idea is good, but the time is bad. People in Port-au-Prince that do not go bare wear sandals, or else they wear sneakers. When Lally or I put polish on their sneaker, they yell like we cut their skin.

We shoeshine boys are too hungry. Some thief organization begins to pay us to hide things in our shoeshine boxes. We collect, run deliveries, carry messages. We learn all the streets and alleys and hiding places, not just in Cité Soleil, but in La Saline, too. Sometimes we carry rice home to Mama, and sometimes we sleep together in some shed where nobody is, or in the *taptaps* where they are parked for the night.

One night we carry the wrong message to some man. I don't know what the message say, but when the man read it, he grab Lally first and beat us hard. So badly, and with no money to pay a doctor, that some people carry us to a church, to Titid's church. . . .

(ଲ

"So this is how you came to meet Titid, Djo?" asks the girl. I see she is reminding me to keep talking.

I nod, and she gives me water, and I can talk again.

(ଲ

This is how Lally and me first come to meet Titid, with bloody noses and swollen eyes like now. Titid was young then, just a young priest starting out, not a famous *Monsieur le President*. In a little office he pull down a box full of doctor stuff and bandage us up. In the courtyard around his church lots of boys hanging out, talking, playing with an old soccer ball.

"If you stay here," one tells me, "somebody will maybe feed you."

Titid comes outside, and the boys gather around.

"Can we sleep in the church, Titid?" one of them asks.

"All you shoeshine boys, you car-shine boys, you street boys, you could make a club and help one another," Titid says.

"Okay, Titid, but where will we sleep?"

"I give you this shed. You fix it up. You can live here."

Lally and I go ask Mama can we stay with the other boys, with Titid. Mama says it is okay, because at home there not be anything for us to eat.

With the other boys that hang around Titid's church, small boys and teenagers, too, we fix up the shed. Put walls and that. It is not easy, because Titid is too pigheaded. Lally and me go to a lot of trouble to steal copper wire from a telephone truck. We peel the wire. We find a street lamp. We run wire into our shed, locate an old socket and pry it loose, beg a bulb. We get the whole thing fixed right, so we all have light at night to play card. What happens? We bring Titid to admire our work.

"You certainly are clever boys, and I am proud to know such. But, you know, it is a wrong thing to steal."

This is stealing?!

But we must take it down.

"Do you think, Jeremie, that is possible to have too much religion at times?"

"Depends what you mean, Djo," she says. She is a hard girl to get in conversation.

"Well, you know, like Titid and this idea we be stealing electric power. Like maybe electric power is something belong to somebody. It comes from his

21

being a priest of the church, and probably he is reading Scripture from the day he is born. See, Jeremie, Titid does not read the Scripture like other priests, who run their eyes across and say the words. Titid worries. 'What do you think this means we should *do*, Djo?' Even when I was still small, he would ask me."

Some other boys at Titid's, Fortuné and Marcel, become our friends. Show us more of the city of Port-au-Prince, even the part up the hill they call Petionville. Tell us car-shine is better than shoeshine.

"People with shoes"—Fortuné shakes his head—"they just pretend they have money. People with cars now, they *do* have money."

"But it is dangerous work," says Marcel. "You have to be quick."

We try it, and I see that what he says is true. We wait on the corner with our rags. When the light turns red, before the car even stop, we jump on the hood. Stretched far across the glass, we begin to rub and polish. Then quick before the light change, we slide down and hold out a hand. Usually the car drive off fast. Sting our fingers against the window. We shout at these drivers, a string of bad words, and they laugh at us.

Lally and I, Marcel and Fortuné, we get to know a few cars that always carry coins for us on the dash.

First day at this work, Lally gets his shorts caught

on the wiper of some Mercedes-Benz. The man inside have on dark glasses. When the light turns to green, he pays no mind to Lally. Could be a fly, you know. Some inconvenience he want to be rid of. He steps on the gas hard; Lally slides to the side of the hood. For a second he is hanging there, upside down, while the car moves fast through the traffic. Then the pants rip, and Lally falls in the dust. The back wheel hits his knee, taking the skin. The car is gone.

I want to talk more, to tell Jeremie everything about us boys. But she says, "Rest now, Djo. I'm punching this thing off, see? Save your story for to-morrow. Sleep now."

Her hand is on my foot, I think.

"Your foot is shaking, Djo. Do you feel it? Your foot is coming to life."

"Jeremie?"

"Yes, Djo."

"You can sing?"

"Ummm."

"So sing me something."

So Jeremie hum a little and rub my feet. I hear that she still too shy to sing right out strong. She hum songs that sound like nun songs.

3

Night again, and I am planning how to tell my story. Jeremie asked me today about living with Titid, about the shelter. She wrinkle her nose a little when she ask, like she think Lafanmi be maybe a nasty place.

I want her to know. I want her to love it like I did.

All we boys are Titid's helpers—Marcel, Fortuné, Lally, all us smaller boys who live in the shelter. Sometime, I hear people say, "Why does Titid trouble with all these good-for-nothing boys?" In your nice way, Jeremie, you ask the same question. So I been thinking on the answer for you.

I think maybe without us Titid would fly away with his too much braininess. The way he grab the hair of a small boy, or lock his elbow around my neck sometime, I know we are not mostly trouble for Titid. We are family. Family is what Titid calls us, and is true. We run errands for Titid, yes. He gets food for us, sometimes even medicine if we sick. But it goes past that only. We are family and also team.

Titid begins to have many friends, all who want to talk to him. And he begins to have enemies, some who want to kill him. When he preaches in the church, the people's love for him is like a big wave: it carries him up, up. But we are there when he comes down, when he is sweaty and weak and needs to be away from the crowd. We are small like Titid. We make a circle around him and we all run off.

People say, "Where's Titid?" and "Some important man must talk with Titid!"

But Titid is gone. We boys have hidden him in a secret place, under the step . . . oh, somewhere, my Jeremie, you know. . . .

Titid does not trust the telephone. He says the government has got a way to listen to his conversation, so it is better to forget the telephone altogether. We boys are his messenger, his telephone with feet. Titid says we must learn all the letters so that we will give the right message to the right man. "Or woman," says Titid, laughing. Then I am glad Eulalie sometimes caught me and Lally, and taught us our letters.

Titid sees what I know, and he says, "Teacher Djo! Tell these boys what sound the letter *D* makes!"

"Duh!" says I.

"Duh! Duh!" yell the other boys, with faces like a political demonstration.

"And what name begins with this letter *D*, boys?" asks Titid, like he's in the pulpit.

"Dessalines!" yells one boy. They all cheer.

"Duvalier!" yells another, in a different voice. They boo.

"Djo!" yells Lally, and all the boys commence their chant:

"D-jo! D-jo!" Like I run for office.

So, Jeremie, Titid assigns me a job. Is to help Pe Pierre, a friend of Titid's, to teach the boys reading. Pe Pierre has a box full of books that he uses to teach the letters and the words. These books are called Taste Salt.

The name makes me remember a story my mama told us. You know this story, Jeremie? How if a person dies, and their body is stolen by a zombie master, the zombie master will make the body rise and work all day and all night as a slave. The zombie understands only his suffering. He has no power to break away. He can only work and work.

But there is one little trick that can save the zombie. Do you remember what it is, Jeremie? Did your mama tell you this?

If the zombie can get a taste of salt, he will understand. He will open his true eyes and see that he has been made a zombie. And he will turn against his

26

master. He will obey him no longer. He will make himself free.

I am not so quick, Jeremie. Among us boys, Lally is the smart one. I use these books with Pe Pierre and not think anything about the title. Then one day I see why the books be called Taste Salt. Is because that is what being able to read and write is like. You understand things you didn't before.

The man I work beside, Pe Pierre, is a Belgian priest, a *blan*. He has worked a long time with *Misyon Alfa* and knows about the big world. I am happy to work with him because he takes time to explain everything to me, to answer every question.

But sometimes I feel like Eulalie herself, pulling ears and twisting arms to make people come learn to read.

"Catch Fortuné, Djo," says Pe Pierre. "Go, bring in Marcel, Djo. I see him peeking in the window making mischief."

I understand now that Titid made me teacher not because I am smart but because I am strong. Most of the boys have a mind to clean windshields all day on the corner, or to beg from the foreign journalists. This is because Titid gave us each a box, with a key, to keep our money in. So, they say, they must earn money to put in the box. To have empty box with key is no good.

I say, "Put your notebook in the box! Put a pencil!"

They look at me like I am crazy.

"Is notebook make big man?" they ask me. "No! Is *money*, Djo. Is *money* make big man."

Or they are busy collecting rocks to throw when we need them. My job is to drag them into class, to make sure they stay there. And is like carrying water in a straw hat, Jeremie.

We need the rocks, they tell me, because Titid has many enemies now. They are right.

Even I make enemies for Titid, Jeremie.

One night, I find the car that dumped Lally, the white Mercedes-Benz. It is parked in front of a night-club. Dance music is coming out loud from inside the club. A pink neon sign is reflecting on the top of the car. The boy hired to guard the car has gone off. I have a razor in my pocket. I stoop behind the car, and I begin to saw the tire. Cutting rubber with the razor is hard. The razor bends and cuts my fingers. Still, after a while the tire sighs and the car settles nicely.

Next night, a black car speeds past the gateway of our church, machine gun blazing. All along our wall are holes. No one is hit.

Titid is not angry with me for this, when I tell him the whole story. He says it is good to have courage to stand up for one another. You know the refrain he uses sometimes in his sermons?

28

The Haitian church is
rich, thanks to the poor,
in a country that is poor
because of the rich.

He reminded me of that.
Titid says that to defend one another, that is wealth.
Solidarity is Titid's big word for it. He writes it on
paper for me. "Put that in your box, Djo," he says
with grin.

   "Is Titid ever angry with his boys?"
   "Oh, yes, Jeremie! Very angry! Is in the same way
that he get angry with his own self."

   One day we are playing street crickets: it is like
cockfights, small-scale. Me and Lally find two crickets.
I pull off feeler from mine, and he pulls off feeler from
his. Now both crickets are riled. Each one is angry at
the other for pulling his feeler off. The crickets are so
small they don't see Lally and me. They do not suspect
us. They do not know we are alive, because we are
too big. So the crickets rush at each other and begin
to fight.
   Lally's cricket needs encouragement, so Lally is yelling. Me, I am down on my knees, praying to my own
cricket to keep the strength. In comes Titid.

"Djo! Lally!" he says, not loud. We jump up. Almost forget the crickets.

"Yes, Titid."

"Is it not a cruel thing you boys do?"

Lally's mouth falls open like a stupid person.

"Why, Titid? Is a game only."

"Only game," asks Titid, "to make two creatures hate and fight?"

"Is only small stupid insect, Titid."

Titid looks at me, and his face is tight because he feel what he say so strong.

"Djo," he says. "Do small stupid insect not be made by God? Do small mean bad?"

4

Whenever I plan what I will say to Jeremie, the question she ask be different from the question I plan for.

"Today," she says, folding her hands like a nun, "I want you to tell me about your political education."

"Jeremie! Was it Titid who tell you to ask me about that?"

She nods. Her eyes laughing now. She does not have to arrange her face to look at me.

"This sound like a Titid question. Or else a foreign journalist question. But okay, I go try.

"Political education. Let me see. . . . What is this thing?"

"Understanding how the country works?" says Jeremie.

"Ooo-eee. You think our country works, then?

The people, yes. Work all the time. But the government? Up until now, it has not worked much."

Jeremie gets serious. "How one thing will influence the other," she says, "and how we can change the way of the thing. Like Titid says, how we might make a decent poor man's life in our Haiti."

"A decent poor man's life. Okay, Jeremie, I give you a test. How does Titid tell it?"

Jeremie smiles and holds out her hand, fingers spread.

"A dry house, with a real roof.

"Clean water to drink.

"A big plate of rice and beans every day.

"Free from curable sickness.

"And working a job—"

"Or working the fields close to home, so families can live together."

"We been listening to the same speeches, Djo."

"Everybody in Haiti been listening to those speeches."

"Is a beautiful dream, Djo, if it can happen. Everybody working for it now. You should see my maman and tantie—"

"So tell me about them, Jeremie. *You* talk today."

"I will, Djo. Sometime. But for now, you tell me about political education."

"All education is political I hear, Jeri."

"That just a Titid answer to a Titid question, you know, Djo."

She is laughing at me. Or maybe is because I call her Jeri. I better stick to what happen.

"Just tell me about working, then, Djo."

"That be a lot easier, Miss *Journalis*."

Washing cars, like I was doing every day when I was nine, ten, eleven, you get to know the people who have cars in the town. There are the people from the high town, the Petionville area, where you see fancy houses like parks and palaces. Those people drive the Mercedes-Benz, sometimes, too, the Porsche and the Jaguar. Most of them be somewhat light-skin. They play-people—go to tennis, to clubs, to disco. They have private servant whose job be only to wash car.

Then there be other rich people, out in Delmas, around there, but they go to work, to office job. They come out early in the morning from their iron gates, go home for siesta, get their car washed maybe on Friday.

Then, you know, Jeremie, you get army people, who have *ti soldat* to wash car and jeep, and *attachés*, a new name for *Macoutes*. They are like military without uniform, to do dirty work. They drive heavy cars such as Isuzu or Cherokee, with tinted glass and window rolled up. We stay away from those.

If there is a new foreigner in Port-au-Prince, the car-shine boys know. The rental cars have a special number on the license plate. Marcel told me right away that rental cars are best for car wash. Most foreigners will give money for car wash from time to time, or before they go turn in the car. Foreigners are interesting to talk to. They always so full of question.

And we car-shine boys get to know the *taptap* drivers. We know the sound of their motor and of their passenger shout, and we jump clear. *Taptap* drivers can teach a lot of political education, Jeremie. They have their car full of people all day long. One or two hundred people in a day. If they have radio, is on full blast. When the news come on, the driver ask their passenger, "What do you think of that?" Or when Manno Charlemagne come on the air, singing one of his songs with the lively tune and the words about maybe what the government doing to the people, the driver sing along. Then he say to the passenger, "Hmmm-mm. He have it about right, don't he? Manno speak the truth, you think?" Something like that to start a conversation.

Oh, yes, Jeremie. *Taptap* drivers hear all opinion. They have some ideas how to make a decent poor man's life. They can spread some ideas, too. . . .

Jeremie has her forehead wrinkled like washboard now. If I could lift my hand, I would smoothe it for her. I tell her instead about Lally. I think she will like Lally.

"Lally does learn and remember all Titid's sermons. Every one. He stands in the courtyard. See him, Jeri? He is the wiry boy with a hole in his shirt. He delivers the sermon to the dogs and the guinea fowl, and to whoever did not hear Titid speak in the flesh or on the radio. We boys call Lally Titid Two."

"Djo?"

"Yes."

"Is this the same Lally, the one the *Macoutes* killed last week?"

She pop the world I am remembering like it a soap bubble.

When I can talk, I say, "Yes, Jeremie. I think is because of what I told you, that we-all call him Titid Two. They kick and kick him, mash in Lally's teeth, I think."

I stop talking because suddenly the girl put her fists before her eyes and lean over to bury her face on the edge of the bed. She stay that way a long time. I wish I could see her, but I can't raise my head.

When she sit up, there are tears in her eyes, but she not shaking.

"I can see him, Djo. I can see Lally like he was, preaching in the courtyard. . . . Okay, Djo. Can you go on? Do you want to tell more?"

I do want to. It is a help some way.

My other work, for Pe Pierre, is mostly twisting arms and toting books. But there, too, Lally help some. Lally is not ashamed to carry the loads of books on his head like a girl.

Our books are very few and tattered, you know, Jeremie. Pe Pierre keeps a box for old newspapers, in French or Creole, some even in Spanish, which is hard to read. Lally and I are what Pe Pierre calls editors. We make lines around interesting news. If it is about somebody we know, we work out the words. Sometimes, the words are not true. Like one day we find a newspaper with headline reading STREET CRIMINALS GIVEN HOME BY RENEGADE PRIEST.

"Who that?" I ask.

"Read on," says Pe Pierre. "Is you boys."

"Cool," says Victor, a big boy. "We be street criminals now. Is your razor cause trouble, Djo."

 One day we find a small article saying FATHER ARISTIDE REPRIMANDED BY SALESIAN ORDER. I have to get Pe Pierre to explain this one. It turns out that the big boss of the church has told Titid to shut up.

Titid calls a meeting at Lafanmi. Titid says to us boys, "What shall I do?"

"Speak," we say.

"But my own church, my Order, which is like my family, too, says, 'Be quiet.' "

Everybody that live at Lafanmi and several others

are at that meeting. Fortuné picking at sores on his feet. Victor looking cool in his dark glasses.

"Take those things off, Victor. I go mistake you for *Macoute*," says Titid. He is not often sharp so. Victor smiles and puts his shades carefully in his pocket. Where did he get them? I wonder. He is big, a man, and Titid takes his advice.

"Do they say, Titid, don't speak anywhere, or do they say don't speak in Haiti?" Victor asks. I admire the question.

"They say, 'Don't speak in Haiti,' " says Titid, looking at the letter in his hand. "Is because I speak out against the government they want me quiet."

"The government doesn't want you quiet, Titid," says Lally, smiling like little angel. "The government want you dead."

Some boys laugh, and Titid smiles, but Victor frowns like he is too important to be interrupted so. He keeps talking as if to Titid alone.

"Then why you not go to the Dominican Republic and speak on radio? Dominican radio reach here in Haiti."

"Yes, but all they put on Dominican radio be D.R. music, *merengue* and such. They not so interested in Haitian politics in Dominican Republic." This is from Alaice, another big boy.

Titid nods.

"Why do you listen to this church Order?" asks Fortuné. "Which is more important—us, or the church?"

"Who do you mean by us?" asks Titid, though he knows.

"Us! Your boys. The people of Haiti. People who want food. People who want work."

"And who or what else?" Titid asks, beginning to relax some. Everybody starts talking at once.

"The peasant cooperatives, the land reform, the Taste Salt class, the *ti kominote legliz*—" People shouting now.

"Everything you been working on, Titid," says Marcel, in a sudden silence.

Titid chews his lip thoughtfully. "I did swear to obey my Order. I did promise obedience."

"But your work, your speeches and all that, they are the more important. To us, they be the real promise."

"The promise to make a new Haiti, like you say," adds Lally.

"I will leave the country," Titid says. "I will try to obey the church. My Order has gotten me an airplane ticket. I will leave this house at ten tomorrow morning."

He walks out. We are left astounded, with our mouths open.

All night we plan, Jeri. It is the first time for me, this working all night, arguing, planning, discussing— designing what the big boys call "action." Every time they say the word, Lally and I take karate chop at each other.

Around the middle of the night, somebody asks, "Who knows all the *taptap* drivers?"

38

Lally and I jump up.

"Okay," says Victor. "Tell everybody to block all intersections between here and the airport. Stall the cars. Pocket the spark plug. Walk in the street. Tell them help us keep our Titid in Haiti. If they have question, or other idea, bring the leaders here."

But he is not talking to us. He is talking to other big boys. We know all the *taptap* drivers. We could go. But he is not talking to us.

Later Alaice says to us, "Go to bed, shrimps. You too small and restless for this work."

But we refuse.

"I got razor," says Marcel. "Can I help?"

"With razor, no," says Victor. "Go find some paint. We need wall signs."

So the big boys write on paper NOU VLE TITID. NUN-LE PO WOM, TITID PO PORT-AU-PRINCE.

"What does it say?" Marcel asks.

"WE WANT TITID. NUNCIO FOR ROME, TITID FOR PORT-AU-PRINCE.

"The Nuncio is the boss man that the Pope send from Rome," explains Victor. "The one that tells Titid to be quiet. The Nuncio is bigwig. He makes trouble for Titid when his job be to help."

"We tell the Nuncio to go home," Alaice says.

We wrote the message on walls all over town, sometimes just part of it before we heard somebody coming. NOU VLE TITID. WE WANT TITID. The important part.

We won.

Titid could not leave. One newspaper reported, RABBLE OF THOUSANDS CHOKES TRAFFIC IN PORT-au-PRINCE.

Titid sent a telegram to his Order. I FIND MYSELF IN THE PHYSICAL IMPOSSIBILITY OF LEAVING THE CAPITAL.

Big words, Titid! True, too.

We wrote a song about it. I drummed. Titid danced with us in the courtyard.

We tape the newspapers onto the wall, down where the smallest boys could try to read them.

"And Jeremie . . ."

She is gone. I wish I did not drift away so. Is such a stupid thing to fall asleep talking.

I see she leave me a yellow flower in a glass by my bed, and a pink one from the banana tree outside. In the middle the pink flower have tiny green bananas.

I wonder what it is like to be Jeremie. I ask her anything about herself, she just smiles and says, "Later." But she listens close to my story. I think sometimes she understands it more than I do. I act so stupid in the next few years, I wonder what she will think.

But I want Jeremie to know. I want her to know what it is like to be me.

40

5

In Lafanmi not one of us knows when his birthday falls. But we know when it is Carnival, when it is Christmas. Four, five years pass since we come to live at Titid's. We all getting bigger. Lally and I still part of Lafanmi, and there be maybe fifty boys now. Titid tries to spend most time with the small ones, who do need him most. Because so many sick people can't pay a doctor, Titid talks somebody into letting him set up the free clinic next to Lafanmi. Then he spend a lot of time driving the sick people around.

Lally and I try and go see Mama and Eulalie and them when we can. We go to the big *bamboche* when Eulalie set up with her boyfriend. My brother Lachaud has shot up tall like me, but Pie stays small and sick with some breathing thing. Emmeline is become pretty like our mama. She has a low belly laugh that surprise you.

For a while now our father stop sending money, and nobody hears from him. Sometimes Mama worries, and other times she angers. Lally and I bring money when we come, so she be extra glad to see us. Mama has a new friend, from up in Cap Haitien, in the north. He a serious fellow and look not too happy to see that our mama has such a big boy as me.

One afternoon we are playing soccer in the courtyard at Titid's, and Lachaud come to tell me Mama is going up north and taking the smaller children. Lally and I clear all the money from our boxes to buy chickens, and go to see Mama. She is laughing and crying, nervous, you know, and tells us she so glad we big boys on our own now. She tell me private if I see my daddy to tell him he a sweet man always. She says she knows he only went away because he had to, for the work. But she can't be waiting her whole life. Is like she telling me she sorry.

When we get back home to Titid's, there is big fuss going on because of all these rumors that somebody want to poison Titid. Titid is receiving bad letters, too. Telephone calls. "We will kill you. Say your prayers, preacher." Things like that.

Lally and I get the dogs to try Titid's food before he eats. So many different people bring him food. Titid doesn't eat much. But we do. We boys always glad to see the line of women with their cook pots.

On the walls where Lally and I painted NOU VLE TITID—we want Titid—someone went and added MOR O VIVAN—dead or alive. We go with paint bucket at night and ex out what they add in, but it make me frightened now when I see the message.

Now come the stupid part, Jeremie. I don't know if I can tell it right. Is very stupid.

In those days everybody else was excited, but not me. Lafanmi did not seem like a family to me anymore. For one thing is become too big. And Titid gone too much. When he not being *taptap* driver for the sick people, he be making speeches. Only the small boys and the boys who are very bad can get his notice when he comes back. Say Morisseau steal something or cut somebody with razor. He always forgiven. And I the one living with this Morisseau. I do wish Titid would do something more than forgive.

When I am teaching the small boys, Titid comes in. Says, "Good work there, Mondestin. Look how smart you be." Or, "Bravo, Morisseau. I glad to see you working so hard." But he forget to say anything to me. Only sometimes: "You got the pencils we need, Djo?" "You think we could maybe clean up this place before photographer get here?"

And the young men, such as Victor and Roger and Alaice, they argue with Titid and make decisions, but they do not listen to my opinion.

I begin to think maybe I am one person too many around Titid's place.

I start to think more about my own daddy, where might he be. He believe in spirit, my daddy, but he be above worry. I think maybe I should go looking for him one day. Deliver the message from Mama. Get some of my daddy's *bamboche* dancer attitude.

How old was I then, Jeremie? I think maybe thirteen, fourteen. Like I say, none of us too sure about our age. I was getting big, I know. And I was getting a devil that made me want to contradict whatever Titid would say. Words flew out of my mouth to argue.

"Djo! Can you carry this message quick to Father Raul?"

"Wait, Titid. I just need to finish this—"

"Djo, the message must go now."

"Okay, Titid." But I tarry for no reason.

"Fortuné, can you carry this message? Thank you, boy. You are a big help," says Titid.

"Titid, I can go," I say.

"Fortuné is gone already. He is quick."

"I am quick."

"Yes, Djo."

"So why didn't you send me?"

"I tried, Djo. It may require a lawyer sometime, to get your help."

This makes me angry. Titid does not like most lawyers. I think he does not like me either. I run into the street.

"You people not need me! You not even want me! If I don't see you again, Titid, is all right with me! Is fine, you hear?"

I want Titid to chase me, but he doesn't. Titid believes in giving a person his freedom, Jeremie. That day Titid leave me free to be stupid. Both of us knowing there are enemies all around. Whether because he angry at the way I been behaving or because he do have true respect for me, I don't know. Titid always leave it to us boys to make our own decisions. . . .

      "Jeremie! You packing up to go? Have I been quiet long?"

"More than quiet, Djo. You been sleeping deep."

"I wasn't asleep, Jeri. I was pondering, you know, pondering on the question of what make freedom." And feeling the sadness of that day. But I not tell her that.

"Djo, you looked mighty sound asleep."

"Is the big questions make a person sleepy, not so?"

Jeremie just smile. Put her hand on my forehead like she check for fever. Swing her bag over her shoulder.

"Come back soon," I say. But I don't know if I say it out loud.

It is night, and I am in the street, somewhere near the port. Still crying like a rainstorm. My body feels too big, and my spirit small as a chick-pea. The street is dark.

I am so tired my head hangs low. I watch my feet fall down—one, then the other. They dirty. I don't see any people on the street.

Tomorrow, I think, I will go back home to Lafanmi, home to Titid. We will forget this foolish argument. Tonight I be too proud, but tomorrow I will go back.

But people are there, on the street. People are lurking in the shadow.

6

Blam! A gunnysack come down over my head.

"He won't bring full fee," I hear someone say.

"He's only a boy."

"Better than nothing."

"And Romain will thank us."

"I hope so!"

Somebody says something in Spanish.

Somebody laughs.

    I feel a rope go around my feet, pulled tight. Hands lift me up rough and throw me down on some board. The board begins to shake. I am in the back of a truck. My shoulder is hurt. Pain rises around me, so sharp and real it is better than the sadness.

Now my mind is a dark tunnel where I go round and round. I feel dizzy and sick. I want to go on through the tunnel, but something is pulling me back. I hear men talking, up above my head.

"Marianne will fret when I don't come home," says a voice.

"Don't worry. You are the lucky one. People in Port-au-Prince fight for this work."

"She will think I am with another woman."

"Untie this boy's feet. Let him sit up here beside me on the bench, where some air can blow on him."

A man is helping me off the floor, pulling my elbow. He sits me on a bench tight between two men. Benches run along the two sides of the truck bed, and on the benches are squeezed maybe twenty men, their knees all mixed together like fingers praying. The truck bed is roofed with a canvas tent. It flaps and shivers in the wind the truck makes. We are moving fast, bumping along, and dust flies in the back in a red cloud, lit by the taillights.

At the back of the truck sits a light-skinned man with a rifle between his knees. He doesn't talk. I think maybe he is the one who was speaking Spanish. Some of the men look dazed, like zombies, they stare so at nothing. But others have open faces, looking at me.

"He will be all right," says one of these, an old man with skin like charcoal wood. "He will cut cane with us, you will see."

I look up. "Cut cane?" I ask.

The light-skin man shifts his gun.

"Is it to cut cane that they take us?"

Everybody looks at me. The old man nods his head and says, "Yes, sonny. We are all going to cut cane in Dominicanie." Another man interrupts him to say, "We leave our dear Haiti to make big money in the Dominican Republic. Is a great opportunity, see?" When he says this, some of the men laugh, but not in a happy way.

One young man looks scared. He stares at the old one, and he says, "Uncle, tell me true. Do we leave our own country? How will we get home?"

The old man shrugs. "That be a problem," he says.

And suddenly, the man who looks so scared jumps up, steps on my knee, and leaps out of the back of the truck. One big scream, a thump, and he is gone in the dust.

The man with the rifle, he stands up quickly, almost loses his balance. He sits down hard, aims his gun into the dust, fires. *Bang!*

I am so surprised, I scream, "You go hurt him, bro'!" And then I know that gun-man aimed to hurt him, kill him maybe. And I know something big is wrong. And I wish Titid or Mama or even Eulalie could come and get me now.

I doze. It is dark outside, moon behind a cloud. Gun-man raps on the cab roof with his rifle stock, and the truck stops. Silence is so deep my ears ring. Gunman looks quick up and down the road. Nobody. No car.

"Out!" he says.

We stumble out.

"Pee!" he says.

Eh-oh. It is ugly how people treat people, not so, Jeremie?

7

"Jeremie! Wake me when you come in. I can sleep anytime. I don't want to miss you."

"I think you've been faraway, Djo."

"You the one always up and gone to the nuns' school. Round the block seem like a long trip to me now."

"Well, see, Djo," she says, "it was just my feet went over there and did the work. *I* stayed here. Waiting and waiting to hear what happen to you next."

Okay, then. The truck stopped. It was light out. We see big mountains that point up sudden, with some few coco trees. We see the sun rise and the big purple sky that stretches out far as bird can fly.

Somebody says, "Border."

Down the mountainside, past a dry river and across the road, runs a coil of silver. It shines like a snake. It is razor wire. On one side, Haiti; on the other, the Dominican Republic.

I turn round and round to see the high mountains, the thick coco trees. The air up here make me feel like a new person. Then somebody grab me by the elbow and push me inside a tin shed. The walls lined with men.

"Sit," the man says.

"Why do we not travel by day?" I ask the driver. He is a Dominican man and talks Spanish to gun-man, but he also talks some small Creole. All day we have been sitting in the shed. No food, no water. It is too hot inside. Back of the truck better than this.

"Too hot to travel," the driver says. He looks at gun-man, and gun-man looks at him. They have some secret.

I say, "Not so hot in the moving truck as in this shed house."

"What for you get so smart?" asks the driver, like he doesn't want to hear my answer.

"I not ask to work in no cane field," I say.

"You are lucky," he tells me. "You get work that many people want."

Hearing this again, it bring a question to my mind.

"If so many people want the work, why do you come and take me with a gunnysack on the street? I—"

Before I can tell them that I already have my work, teacher work, *paf!* The gun-man slaps me upside the face with the flat end of his rifle. My jaw cracks. I spit blood. If I feel like talking now, my tongue be too fat.

Djo, I tell myself, you've got to get your tail out of this mess. So I watch the door of the shed. But gun-man watches me. And I am not going anywhere.

Jeremie, I just sitting there, fist in my mouth, thinking that Djo be some fine fool. And these other men in the shed feel even worse than me, because they are grown men. They don't look at one another. They look past, at nothing, or they pretend sleep.

All except the old man.

"What's your name, uncle?" I ask. I need to know somebody, at least somebody's name.

"Dieudonné. They calls me Donay."

"Have you been here before, Donay?"

He smiles a tired smile and nods his old head. His eyes have gray fog on them, but he looks at me direct.

"Tell me, Donay," I ask him. "Tell me what is happening here."

"They have sold you, boy," he says softly. "These people that put you in the truck have sold you as worker to the boss of a *central*."

"And Donay," I say, hardly able to speak, "what is a *central*?"

"Is a place that grows sugar."

"Is it for my life, Donay?"

Donay hesitates. He looks down at his feet; then he looks again at me. "It is only for the season, sonny. Just be careful you not fall into debt. For then they do own you."

How would I fall into debt? I wondered. Making big money in the Dominican cane fields, a boy could not fall into debt. I would work a season and buy shoes for our mama. Buy Titid an honest light bulb. Thinking on this, I begin to feel better.

"Is it hard work, Donay?"

"Very hard, sonny."

"Do you make big money?"

Donay looks sad. "I have worked many years in the cane field. Money? No." Donay shakes his head slowly, a long time, like he can't figure it. "I live, sonny. It's all a man can do." He gives a shrug, like a shiver went over him. Donay puts his hand on mine. It feels light and dry and scarred. Like a cornhusk.

How is it possible for Donay to have worked so long and never make money? Soon enough I find out.

 Nightfall comes. My belly feels like our soccer ball at Titid's, got no air but people kick it anyway. Gun-man kick open the shed door.

"You have money?" he asks.

Stupid question. How would we get money, sitting on our backsides in a shed?

"We must feed you, and you need to pay."

"We not ask to be here," I say. And *paf!* There goes the other side of my face.

"When will you learn to keep quiet?" asks gun-man, just as I am thinking the same thing.

"Okay, well," says gun-man. "We are nice people here. We will let you buy on credit. A man bringing your rice just now. You tell the man your name, and he will give credit to you."

We are so hungry. How are we going to ask questions, like what is credit?

Later, in darkness, they bring us out and push us back on the truck.

I want to see this Dominican Republic, but I am too tired. The truck bounces, dust flies, canvas flaps, and Djo sleeps. So I don't see the cane field until next morning, when gun-man nudges me with his rifle and says, "Get down, boy. You have arrived. Welcome to Central Gloria, your new home."

The sunlight blinds me, and my legs are not working too good, but I try to stand straight.

This cane field business appears at first to have just two colors: a too-big blue sky, and a too-much green cane, growing like giant grass. We are on a path between tall cane, feeling small as crickets. The cane tops shake in breezes, but no breeze reaches down here.

Why did they leave us here? There is nothing on

this path. No house, no store, no car, no person. Nothing. The driver starts the truck motor. Gun-man gets in the cab. He waves his rifle at us. "Walk that way," he says. "Go on!" And so the truck leaves us.

 "Enough for tonight, Djo," says Jeremie. "You are sounding like an old frog. I want to get some *tisane* of chamomile for your throat."

I am watching her go. She stops at the curtain, turning back toward me.

"Djo," she says. "Don't go dreaming your story all by yourself. I want to hear it."

Okay, Jeremie, okay. So I think of her instead. I like the way she knows how I am feeling. I like the way her mouth changes from serious to funny.

8

"**Y**ou come ask for rice and beans like some big shot *bracero*, eh? Look at the small boy who thinks he's a man!"

The *colmado*-man, who runs the *colmado* store, doesn't even get up. The *colmado* is the only store on this settlement, a little island of shacks in the middle of an ocean of cane. The only place to get food.

The *colmado*-man is slapping dominoes with other men, and they are laughing. A small pig with runny nose trots by my foot, snuffling some old orange peel. The pig is my brother, not the man.

"But I will work," I say. "Give me half a cup of rice only, and I will pay you soon."

"Look how the boy wants credit, now," says the *colmado*-man.

"Have heart," I say.

"Okay," says *colmado*-man. "I have children, too. I have heart. I give you your half cup of rice today, but you must put your X here, and here—double credit for the boy who doesn't work yet."

The *colmado*-man pushes a worn notebook across the counter, full of scribbled numbers, names penciled over, X's, shaky signatures.

I find a space and I write carefully, *½ cup rice, Djo Leguardien*.

The *colmado*-man narrows his eyes at me.

"What day today?" I ask. When he tell me, I write that, too. The *colmado*-man make a noise sucking on his teeth. He pull back the notebook and mark a big 1 over top the ½. I see that he seriously means to charge me double. I am plenty angry, Jeremie, but there is nothing I can do.

Tomorrow, I think. Tomorrow I start work. Make money. Pay off credit. I will work with Donay's team. He told me so.

Next morning one light-skinned *central* boss lines us up and looks us over.

"You are too inexperienced to cut cane," he says, pointing at me where I stand next to Donay, "and he's too old. Both you work on Lagurie's team."

I find out too late that nobody wants to work with Lagurie because he is a mean *sansmaman*. This is why Lagurie has no team already. Everybody that can has quit Lagurie's team. Donay knows, but I see Donay accepts everything, like rain, like sun. Donay is like some old saint Titid told me of. He works. He doesn't vex. He is a better man than me.

But Donay does not think to tell me to beware of this Lagurie. I have to learn that for myself.

Fresh cane is heavy. It has a prickly surface and it has sticky juice. When I get juice on my skin, red ants come. Why do they sting me so? Why don't they eat the sugar that runs on the ground?

Lagurie is a good cutter, I give him that. With his big back shiny with sweat, he swings the machete low and cuts the cane close to the ground. And each time he gives a grunt.

Whap! Hunh.
Whap! Hunh.
Like so. He never stops.

Donay's job is to go behind Lagurie and arrange his cane. Donay pulls out the cane and straightens it in stacks. Then I come and drag each stack up to the track, so the *charette*-man can pick it up. The *charette*-man will come by with an oxcart; then we will all load; then the *charette*-man will take the cane to the weigher, at the *central*. Donay tells me this. But I haven't seen this *charette*-man all day.

Cane is heavy, like I say, but I am anxious to prove a good worker. I don't complain, even to Donay. But Lagurie, he does complain, plenty.

"Why do they give me such a thin young boy to

haul my cane?" he asks the sky. "Why do they burden me with a useless old grandpa?"

Donay is so gentle, he does his job and says nothing. It is very hot, working. It is up to Lagurie to call a break, since he is the team boss. Lagurie doesn't call any break. I am so tired from bending to drag the cane, I think, Djo, you are going to fall down and die, beginning with your backside.

Lagurie has a gallon jug of water. It is plastic, swollen up tight in the sun. Lagurie takes a swig from time to time, with a loud gulp. By high sun, I get dizzy. I can lean down, but I can't straighten up.

"Lagurie," says Donay. "The boy go fall."

Lagurie makes a bad face. Only now he offers me water, his hot dirty water he been spitting in all day. "Not too much," he says.

"This *charette*-man slow today," grumbles Lagurie. "He wants the cane to be so dry it weighs like chaff. *Central* pays him to be so slow."

I look to Donay for an explanation. "They pay the cutter by the weight of the cane," says Donay. "So much for each ton. The sun makes the cane light-light."

I am sweating hard. The sweat run in my eyes and in my mouth, and I taste salt. I see now what is being done to us, to Donay, to Lagurie.

The anger begins in me. It stings more sharp than red ants. Inside, you know. Inside the spirit. And I remember what Titid said. Something, somebody out there so big I cannot see them, somebody doing this to us.

I tell myself, Keep going, Djo. Tonight you get paid, get off the credit, be your own boy again. I am so dizzy my two feet look like four. Can't think, can't count. Eulalie be ashamed of me. Still, I have hope. Foolishly.

It turns out that nobody gets paid, except Lagurie. And all he gets is one small piece of paper that the *charette*-man give him.

"It is good for use at the *colmado*-store," explains Donay.

"For us, or only just for Lagurie?" I ask. I am so hungry I am past being hungry. I begin to understand why Donay is so calm. It's because he has no strength for anger. His answer comes very quietly.

"It is for Lagurie only. Only the cutter gets paid. But Lagurie, he will buy us small rice for our help."

Small rice, I think, for big work. And I will still be in debt for the credit. Still owe the *colmado*-man two for one for every grain of rice I did already eat.

It is better to be a shoeshine for people who don't wear shoes. Or even a thief.

Titid says the thief hurts himself. That the thief is not a proper man.

And all these thieves in the *central*, are they not ashamed? The *charette*-man, *colmado*-man, gun-man. Lagurie himself. Is Donay the only proper man here?

And I think, too, and I feel bad to think this, Jeri, but I ask myself, Is Donay himself a proper man? Is he the way man should be?

Know where they put us to sleep, Jeremie?

It is a concrete barn. It is too wet in there, and people cough. The workers who have some friends among the bosses, they get pieces of cardboard to sleep on. When the cardboard becomes too wet, they get another. Donay tells the *central* guard I will sicken if he does not give me cardboard. He tells the man I will fall sick and cost money to fix, and because of that the man gives me a piece of cardboard. I see the man doesn't give Donay one. And I believe now that the man doesn't care if Donay falls sick, because Donay is past his hard-work years. And Donay, he knows that, too.

He and I turn the cardboard sideways. We both put our head and arms on the cardboard, but our legs are on the concrete.

"You shaking, Djo," says Jeremie, and her voice is different, scared. I feel so cold suddenly; yet I feel a shaking all over like fever or earthquake. Jeremie rises to go for help, but I hold on to her. I feel the bones in her hand.

9

I don't know what all I have told Jeremie. Something happened, I think. Somebody been sponging my face. Somebody call the doctor. Somebody give me an injection.

I have been so deep asleep I thought never to crawl back up. Is hard to breathe now.

"How you feel, Djo?" She is here, right by my head. Was her voice, then, that woke me.

"Like bag of sand, girl, only worse. . . ."

"The doctor coming, Djo." She touches my face with the back of her fingers.

 The doctor comes in. He looks at me disgusted. I am wasting his good work.

"Djo," he says, "you have been talking again. You

talk too much. You get excited. You get angry. This"—he waves toward Jeri or maybe her recording machine—"this is not good for you. You must rest.

"Anger uses up your strength," he says.

And he says, "You might live, Djo. But you need every scrap of your strength." He means that I might die, any time.

"If I don't talk," I try to tell him, "then I die completely."

But the doctor either doesn't hear, or he doesn't understand. Because he says, "Don't talk, Djo."

The doctor puts a tube in me. Liquid drips down from a bag and goes inside my arm. "Is very modern medicine," he says. "It feeds you sugar."

Sugar! I feel my heart pump. Sugar going into my arm? People say cane juice is good for everything, from manness to dreams. "Cane juice goes into my arm so?"

"Cane juice, water, salt. And vitamins," says the doctor.

I see Jeremie smile about the vitamins. I am glad that she smiles, because her eyes are sad today, and I think she is always here when she needs sleep. She smiles because we have been hearing a song on the radio from the street corner, a *merengue* song from the Dominican Republic. All day long the song been saying, "Tender affection is the vitamin of life. . . ."

"Djo has vitamins," Jeremie says softly, as if to the doctor.

I see that she means she has affection for me. And is true I feel it. Is like a wave of calm strength go through me.

"Good," says the doctor, but he doesn't look happy. "Djo needs them." And he leaves.

"Jeremie," I say, just to hear the name. And then, to say something, I go on.

"If that stuff be sugar, where are the red ants?" My voice comes out a whisper.

"Djo," says Jeri, leaning toward me, "your bed is standing in four tuna cans full of water. From where the ant sit, you are living on an island."

I like this idea some.

Jeremie takes my hand in both of hers. I get a surprise. Her hands are very rough, scarred. Is strange, because her face is so smooth and young. Her hands be like hands of an old person, like Donay's own.

"Jeri, why your hands so rough?"

She catches her breath, and I am sorry I asked.

"You been stripping palm, Jeremie?"

"Yes, Djo," she says, looking relieved. "Is one of my jobs, you know."

"Jeremie."

"Yes, Djo."

"Will you come onto my island?"

She will not sit on the bed. She stays in her chair, where she can see my face. She looks at me seriously, and she says, "Djo, I have been living on your island for six days now. It is the only place I live."

She begins to cry.

"Stay," I say.

"You stay, too," she says. "Please, Djo."

10

The guards at Central Gloria call us *kongos*. It means that we be straight from Africa. The guards, they use the name *kongo* for insult. But my father always did speak of Africa as a place to be proud of, a place he dream about. Most every insult the guards use against us is two-sided. It have inside it something to be proud of, but is confusing, too.

Listen, girl, to what we hear every day.

"Only *kongos* will work all day in the hot, hot sun."

"*Kongos* are strong."

"*Kongos* are stupid."

"*Kongos* don't complain."

"*Kongos* are proud."

"*Kongos* are stupid."

They say these things always as insults.

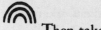 Then take a look at Donay.

All those things the guards say, they are true of Donay. Donay is proud. Look how he does his work so well, how he lines the cane carefully, evenly, straightening the broken places so all the juice does not flow out. Look how he moves quickly to stay out of Lagurie's way. Look how he says kind, polite things, how the old greetings, "Honor," "Respect," come naturally to him even here at La Gloria.

Donay is stupid. He makes his mind tough, closed against insult, closed against meanness. What say, Jeremie? Proud, yes. When Donay is stupid, it is a kind of pride. He does not let himself be angered by meanness.

Donay is strong, though so very old. The whole day he does not sit down. He moves carefully, slowly, but he never stops. He does what needs to be done. Even when Lagurie calls a rest, Donay is there with the sharpening stone and puts an edge on Lagurie's machete. With strong strokes he pulls the blade against the stone, sharpening it.

 Donay and I are both too tired to talk while we work. Sometimes, though, in the evening when we are waiting for a little rice to cook, we talk.

I ask Donay why he was on the truck with me. If he did get away from the *central*, then why did he come back? Donay tells me that at the end of the last

69

zafra, the *central* boss did tell all of the workers who were old or sick they must return to Haiti. Trucks came and took them to the border. Donay was one of the ones that the boss put on the truck. This is how he told me his story, Jeri.

"**I** get off the truck, Djo, back in Haiti at last after so many years. I am full of joy: I will see my children again—my two daughters who were children when I left. I walk many days, asking after them. As I walk, my knees tire. I grow more hungry and stop often to cough.

"I think to myself, I wish I had presents for my daughters, to make their life more easy. I wish I did bring school fees, and gifts for my grandchildren. All I do bring is myself.

"And I think, I am old now. My strength is gone, used up in the cane field. My daughters, they be grown now. Each one with children and maybe grandchildren of her own. For what do they need an old man like me, to eat from their pot and be a burden to them when he turns sick?

"After a week I so hungry I must stop often to lean against tree or building. I get to Port-au-Prince. Down at the market I see the truck from Dominicanie, and the recruiter looking for workers. I watch him, talking to the young men, the boys, promising much. I stand tall, make myself look strong. I hold back the cough,

and while he not looking hard, I climb on the truck
again."

When Donay tell me this, Jeremie, I want family. I want him to be my family, and I want to be his family. We stuck here together in this place, both so all alone. Is like I want to make up for all the sad leaving behind—my daddy that leave us, my mama that leave me, Donay that leave his daughters, me that leave Titid and the boys.

I try to tell Donay about Titid. About Lally and Fortuné and Marcel.

"I would like to meet those boys," says Donay. "I would like to hear that priest." Staring off across the cane, Donay says, "You know, Djo, I am Haitian. Yet I don't know anybody in Haiti now."

"They will want to know you, Donay. They will be proud to know you."

Donay keep staring, and I think he need some convincing, so I say, "Will you come with me, Donay? We will go together to Titid, and you will be his helper, like us. You will be cook, which he needs. You will be grandfather, Donay, which we do all need." I tell Donay about the clinic Titid just starting, this clinic we in now, Jeremie. "If you fall sick, Donay," I tell him, "it will be easy to care for you."

And I think, Surely there is a way to escape from this *central*, from this Dominicanie. Surely there is a way to get back to Haiti.

"Djo," says Donay, shaking his head as he does when he knows I hope too much, "you and I cannot leave the *central*. Unless they do send us out."

"Why not, Donay?"

"There are paths through the cane, Djo, but guards patrol these with guns. And then many long roads. On the roads, people will see us, and they will know us to be Haitians. They will ask for our papers, and when we do not have any, they will throw us in jail and then bring us back here."

"How will they know we are Haitians, Donay?"

"By the color of our skin."

"But Dominicans, too, are black. Some of them. . . ."

Donay smiles gently, almost proudly. "Black, yes. But not so black as us. Not so very, truly black."

"But Donay, if they stole us away to work, they know we cannot have papers."

"They stole us away to work, Djo, and that is all they want us to do. If we do not work, they would prefer for us to be dead."

When he said that, Jeremie, I remembered the man who jumped off the truck. Gun-man shooting into the dust. I knew it was true.

But, I thought, Donay and I know cane. We can make our way through the cane away from the paths.

We can hide from the guards. We can eat cane, drink the juice.

"Isn't it true that Dominicanie and Haiti share one island, Donay?"

"One long, long island, Djo."

"Then if we watch the sun, we can always go west. If we go west, we will come to Haiti."

"Except, Djo, when the sun is high and confuses the mind."

"That's when we will rest, Donay."

Donay, squatting, adjusts our tin can of rice, which hangs over the fire on a piece of wire. It is his invention for cooking, and he is proud of it. But we have to be careful. We are burning old cane stalks, and they burn fast. Donay smiles his old man smile, like a child listening to a story.

"How long does the cutting season, the *zafra*, last?" Jeremie asks.

"Maybe six months. At first I all the time telling myself, You can do it, Djo. For six months you can do this work. Six months is not so long."

"But then?"

"Jeremie, it turn out that those men who put the gunnysack over my head, those people who sold me to the *central*, what they have be a one-way operation. They take workers to Dominicanie, yes, but they don't bring them back."

One night after I been hauling cane for so many weeks that my hands are like leather, I go to the *colmado* as always for a cup of rice to feed Donay and me.

"Hey, boy!" says the *colmado*-man. The counter is crowded with tired and hungry men, and they all look at me as I look at the store owner. He is Dominican, but he speaks Creole when he wants to.

"When are you going to pay off your debts?"

"When the *zafra* is over and I get my bonus. When it is time to go home." I feel good saying the word. But there is a laugh from the men at the counter, the same uncomfortable bitter laugh I first heard on the truck.

"You plan to go home, boy?" asks the *colmado*-man.

I nod, but a shiver of fear is going up my back.

"How many of you *kongo* boys will be going home this year?" asks the *colmado*-man. The men at the counter shrug. No one says, "Me!" No one waves a hand.

"How long have you been in Dominicanie?" the *colmado*-man asks one of the men at the counter.

"Six years," he mumbles.

"And you?"

"Ten years."

"And you?"

"I was born here."

"Oh, Djo," says Jeremie, her forehead like washboard again.

"So you see, Jeri, that I had to plan an escape, for me and for Donay. Or that's what I thought, even though I think Donay was past caring. He was coughing more and more. Those other men at the counter—I guess they had hoped one time, too. I knew that if I waited even one more day to make plans, I might lose my will."

"Lose the taste of salt," Jeri says.

I was thinking that.

"But you just not the zombie type, Djo."

"I think no person be the zombie type, Jeremie. Nobody born fit to be a slave."

For a while we don't say anything. Jeremie just rubbing my feet the way she does, without even thinking, now. Then she change mood. Her face smooth out.

"You know, Djo, the doctor think you got a little too much taste of salt. So drink water now. I will sing you to sleep. The rest of the story can wait till tomorrow."

And she rub my feet and sing her little nun songs, and pretty soon I feel like I back in the rocking chair.

11

There is a boy at Central Gloria named Julio. He is Dominican. He is hired to watch the paths, to make sure none of we Haitians escape. I notice him because he carries his rifle like a guitar. Leaning against a wall of the *colmado*, he strums the stock with eyes shut, singing songs to himself under his breath.

Watching Julio, I see how restless I would be, except I am always so very tired.

One evening after the work is done, I find Julio off duty, leaning against the wall, playing a real guitar. I sit down near him with a burned cook pot. I pick up a stick and I put a *merengue* beat underneath the song Julio singing. He stops playing, looks at me, begins again. After that we spend time together most every evening. He strums chords; I drum decoration. He plucks notes like waterfall; I put in the beat. Sometimes we talk.

Because I befriend a Dominican, a guard at that, some workers look at me with suspicion.

Marricon! Lagurie hisses at me. Suck-up!

But it is not like that. I ask Julio some questions.

"Why do you work here, guarding people like they be thieves?"

"I hate it," says Julio.

"Why do it?"

Julio rubs his fingers together.

"Do you earn much?"

"Very little."

"Do you save any?"

Julio shakes his head.

"Why stay?"

He shrugs. He answers me with a song about no work, all the places he try, all the jobs that come to nothing. A good song. I think it be the song of many Dominican people. We give it a *merengue* beat. A person who not listen to the words never know that it be a sad song. . . .

"How did you talk with Julio, Djo?" asks Jeremie.

"Julio had lived half his life among us *kongos.* He could understand Creole without thinking, and speak it, too. And you know, Jeremie, how we always hear

Dominican radio on the street here in Haiti. I knew songs by heart in Spanish. Like you, Jeri. You understand the songs."

Jeremie looks out the window. She not want me to see the smile on her face.

"Mostly Julio and I just sing together, make music, drum."

"You are good at that, Djo."

"What?"

"Singing. Drumming."

"When did you hear me sing, Jeremie?"

"In the church. And one time when we marched to Fort Dimanche in demonstration."

"You were there, Jeremie? Is this true? How can you be keeping secrets from me when I am telling you my entire life?"

"You gonna hear from me, Djo, don't worry. Just tell me one thing. Did you play Julio's guitar?"

"No. I never played Julio's guitar, though I did want to."

"Why not?"

"The reason?"

The reason is something like this.

In the *batey*, we *kongos* are considered like donkeys, to be worked. To be more than that is to make trouble.

Say a man have donkey he likes, Jeri. Is nice donkey and sings pretty good. So the man say, "Okay, you donkey, you can sing with me." But if the donkey sing better than the man, then watch out! Donkey Djo learn to act slow. Because inside, teacher Djo be thinking fast and careful.

One night the guards pass round a bottle of rum. Julio gets the bottle. Without thinking, he holds it toward me. I like to try the rum. No. I shake my head just brief. I look away. Because if I drink, some of the guards be angry. Some not drink after a *kongo*. Some make Julio lose his job. And donkey Djo needs Julio.

Do you see, Jeremie? The slave needs to be stupid and quick, carefree and careful. Is hard work. Harder even than cutting cane.

"Okay, yes, you are right, Jeremie. I need to be still and stop pulling this stupid tube in my arm. I begin to be riled. Is because I am ashamed, Jeri, ashamed. Julio deserved better. He did not treat me like a donkey. And I did treat him like a guard. . . .

"Can you find me water? Look, Jeremie, how that small lizard walks on the top of the banana leaf outside. How the sun shine on him and cast such a clear, fine little shadow. . . ."

12

"No. I am not sleeping. Only thinking here inside. Thank you for the water, Jeri. Is like movie theater inside my eyes. Here. I give you a free ticket. I invite you, Jeremie."

See the *batey*, the dirt road leading through, the shacks made of cornstalks roofed with banana leaves. I share one of these with Donay now. Together we have made pallets of cane chaff and leaves. They look like a picture Eulalie show me once, where they did put the baby Jesus to sleep. In the picture were little white sheep. In the *batey* we have instead black rats.

See the concrete barn where workers live, the small church with tall voodoo drums for calling spirit, the wash flapping, women roasting peanuts, men slapping dominoes, pigs running here and there.

All around walls and miles of cane, blowing in waves like the ocean off Port-au-Prince. In some way, at some times, it is beautiful.

Two things bother. Hunger and Anger. We are here by trickery. We work hard and never eat. Never enough to stop the hunger. Hunger and Anger are like two dogs, two thin mean dogs that follow me. I check sometimes to make sure they still there. Hunger and Anger be like salt. I do not want to lose them, Jeremie. They will help me get out of here.

A good walk from the *batey*, behind the latrine, is a ditch. Irrigation canal, they call it. The Dominican government has used much concrete to make this ditch, to bring water to the cane fields when the rains fail.

One night I am knocking rhythms from the pot, and Julio plucking guitar. Somebody bring up the ditch.

"It is many miles long," says Julio. "Took seven years to build." Then he looks at me in a funny direct way, poking me awake with his eyes. "It comes all the way from the mountains."

He plays chords. He makes up song.

> *"All the way, moving, moving*
> *from the mountains*

> *through the road of concrete*
> *comes the water.*
> *From the mountains of Dajabon*
> *of Haiti*
> *bringing water to the cane field*
> *the sugar. . . ."*

And Jeremie, my neck shivers and my hair stands up taller. I know that Julio is telling me how to escape the *central*. Wade in the water, Djo, Julio is telling me. Follow the ditch up to Haiti.

Next day I listen for talk of the ditch.

"Is poison water. Is bad water from the ditch that make my baby belly swell so," says Marie, Lagurie's woman, carrying her youngest on her hip, her child sad with bellyache.

"Is like a web of roads. Is entire canal system. One canal leads to crossing place and meets with another," explains one man Bernard, drawing lines in the dirt with a stick.

"Pesticides make ditch water bad," says Lagurie. "Filthy poisons. The government not going to trouble to keep the ditch clean, because the people who live along the ditch are all *kongos*."

"So there are many *kongos* living along the ditch?"

"Who else would work the rice fields, the tomato fields, the cane fields, little stupid?"

It was the first time I knew about those other fields, Jeremie.

"Dirty *kongos*," says a guard. "Bathing, pissing,

82

washing, drinking, all in the same water. No wonder they get sick."

That night Julio complains of his job. Usually he never does complain right out loud, so I listen.

"Every night I am right here," says Julio. "No radio, no new face, no nothing. Only Tuesday they give me off, and Tuesday nothing happening. No party, no music, no girls, no ride to town. Then they give me this good-for-nothing rifle. Ammo next week, they say. Three months ago. So I can't shoot even a rat. The other guards, after dark, they are so drunk a *baca* crash through the cane and they not hear. . . ."

The plan comes together. Donay and I must go out by the ditch, at night after dark. Any night but Tuesday be okay.

"Donay!" I whisper to him, while everyone sleep. "We can do it! We have a plan. Listen. . . ."

Donay start to answer and then he start to cough and when he can talk again he say, "Is a good plan, Djo. Only thing is, if I slip under the water, I go drown, because I never did learn to swim."

"The water not deep, Donay. And anyway, we don't have to stay always in the ditch. Is just to get past guards. Other times we can walk along, you know."

Donay is too old and too weak to wade in poison water.

For Donay, I think, for Donay we need a raft. Donay cannot swim, and already his cough is bad. There is some sickness taking his strength. If I had a raft, I could push Donay.

Then one night come Julio with crate from *central* machinery.

"Don't touch that crate," he says loudly. "That crate is not for *kongos*. In two days man come fetch that crate. If it not be here, some *kongos* be in bad trouble!"

Later I have a chance to look at the crate closely. It is strong, tight. It will work fine for a raft. It will carry Donay, if I swim behind and not tip him. Two days, I think. Thank you, Julio.

I act angry with Julio so no one suspect that he help us. "Why you not let us use that crate for a bed? It make good bed."

"Is not for you, *kongo*," says Julio. No, I think, is for Donay, and Julio knows that.

Next day I hear Julio talking to another guard. "Somebody needs to inspect the bank of the ditch. Too much trash and stuff in there. It's those damned *kongos*. Maybe is best to find some old *kongo* to inspect the ditch, some old man that is not too useful in the *zafra*. Give him uniform cap."

84

Julio goes off, comes back with gunnysack. Inside, Jeremie, be a cap such as the *central* guards wear. A treasure, Jeri.

That day, Jeremie, I am so happy I drag cane like angel, like superman. I am fast; I am magic; I have wings to work. I am going home. I must snap my jaw tight to keep the song inside, so Lagurie not suspect. When Lagurie lend me his machete, I cut cane like helicopter blade—*Whap! Whap! Whap!* To every side cane flying. Was a fine day, Jeremie.

Aie, Jeremie. Here come the doctor with his too serious face. Better I sleep now. Better I tell you the story tomorrow. Tonight, like me, you can dream of the escape. Of Donay on the raft and me swimming behind, swimming against the current, up into the mountains, up to Haiti.

13

"Djo! Mornin', Djo. I'm waking you, Djo, like you said to do."

"Jeremie. You here already?"

"And you dozing still."

I only just now went to sleep, Jeremie.

"You are ready to hear about our escape? Your recorder machine is turning?"

Tuesday pass like *bamboche*. Our plan to leave Wednesday night. Every time I see Donay, I want to hug the man. He so old and sweet, and we have secret.

But Wednesday evening Donay coughs. Is a deep, hard cough worse than what had been. I go to help him and see he cough blood. There is death in this cough.

He knows, and I know, is his time.

"Go without me, Djo," he says. "Be my legs, Djo."

He takes my hands as if to push me, push me away. But there is fear in him, too. Without knowing it, he clings to my hand. Tight. Like my little brother Pie when he have a bad dream.

I stay by Donay. The night go by very slowly. I dream about escaping. Is dream only.

I wake up to see the pink light of day. It shines through the banana leaves of our hut, shines on the dust. It makes patterns of light shaped like birds.

Be my legs, Djo.

Be my wings, Donay.

Donay's head is on my arm. His two hands are holding my hand. Donay is dead. I let go of the fingers. They do not feel like Donay's fingers anymore. Just used fingers, you know. His body is curled the way my little brother Pie used to sleep. But all the spirit gone.

I sit there thinking, Jeri. Thinking at first about the chance to go home. I could do it still. Easier, in some way, without Donay. Thinking about home, about Titid and Lally and them. Thinking about home before that, about my father. About the picture of Christ and what my father say about the Go-between. And I wonder, do the Go-between have to be one person, like white Jesus in the picture? Or can the Go-between be any person, any good, gentle person, like Donay?

And then I come back to thinking about Donay,

and how all his life he is used and thrown out like he not important, like he not the best. About how in truth he *be* the best, Jeremie.

I ask to put Donay's coffin on credit at the *colmado*. The *colmado*-man raise his eyebrows high, hesitate a second, then say yes. The *colmado*-man takes me to town in his car, to choose. He have the only car on the *batey* except for the *central* boss's and the trucks. It is the first time I ride inside a car other than *taptap*.

At the coffin store the owner and the *colmado*-man look at each other in a funny way, but I used to this by now. The coffin is expensive. The man explain how it very fine. Though I do notice it have some scratches, and that the two screws on the handle not match up. Still, it is fancy and solid, and the man say it be the best.

I sign my name next to a number with many zeros, to promise payment. It make a weight in my bones to do it. At the same time, Jeremie, I am glad to, since it be something for Donay.

The wake is in the evening, after the others come off work. Everybody crowd into the small church. Donay's body is there in the middle, shrunk in the big coffin, looking lonely to me. My hand move to stretch out and touch again, and fall back. There be no comfort through the body anymore.

All we people in there try to touch through the spirit. One man I always see swinging machete is leading the service, singing with eyes closed, calling down the spirit. One other man, I don't know his name even, come touch me on the shoulder.

"Is good thing you do for our brother, boy. I go put my name beside yours."

A woman come up, tears on her face, say, "We go help, too, boy. We all of the same blood."

Beside me, Lagurie's woman, Marie, stand praying, tears down her face, the baby pulling at her breast.

I am no longer all alone among strangers.

We all in this together. Titid had a big word for it. I try to think of it, but it is gone.

Other thoughts push in my mind. How there be two kinds of freedom. The one kind I already did know about, had a taste of at Titid's, and before, too, with Lally. That was a run-around freedom that seem faraway to me now—freedom to make your plan, drum on the shoeshine box, earn a little money, buy a chicken, read the paper. But the other kind, when I think about how in time I will be dead, it seem more true. That be freedom from worrying what to do for Djo. That the kind of freedom Donay had always. Donay not think about himself. And I think if I can find Donay's kind of freedom, then I will be ready for the other kind. Be ready to use it right.

"Drum, boy," somebody say, and they push me through the people to the tall drum.

So I drum, drum, drum. Take all the pain and sadness I feel, drive the pain down through the drum into the earth. The earth take it, understand it, send it back up through our bare feet, through our body and moving and song, all the people feeling the pain there together make the earth ready for the body, try, try, try to send the spirit on its journey, like Donay's spirit be our own, which it is that day.

The wake go all night, till the sun come up, and when it is over, I not even allowed to go with Donay's body to the burial ground, which is outside the *central*.

"Already you lose too much work," says the *central* boss.

At noon, working without Donay, Lagurie and me stop, share water, chew cane. What day it be? I wonder. What difference do it make? I look at the cut cane lying around, and I bend over, untangle a mess of it. Carefully and neatly I line up the cane, straightening the broken places. I do not want to leave. For now I need to stay.

"But Djo, what do you do between one *zafra* and the next?"

"There is always some work, Jeremie. . . .

"You want to know what kind? After the *zafra* over, I work on drainage ditches for rice, I clear weeds,

I cut and burn chaff. I help clean the *ingenio*, with its heavy creaking machine that crush the cane. I clean the black oil that crust on the conveyor belt and rollers and teeth. I paint on new black oil. I get the machinery ready for the next *zafra*."

"You sweating, Djo. You feel worse now? You want me to call the orderly?"

I don't like that machine. Is like a monster to me, and if I hear it in a dream, then I know is time to wake up and listen to the rooster.

"Is okay, Jeri. Don't worry."

"What happened about the coffin, Djo? Did you and those others pay for it all?"

I been talking enough today, Jeri.

"Your foot going crazy, Djo. Is not a good idea to move so. I am scared you will lose the IV, Djo. Oh, somebody! Come quick! We have trouble here!"

Jeremie's voice come from far away. I feel big fire in my chest and then all over, and when I try to put it out, something pull loose, make it worse. I gone up a tunnel. Hurricane come sweeping down for me. . . .

II · JEREMIE

14

I waited too long. I wanted to answer Djo's questions, to tell him about me. But I told myself it would do him more good to tell his own story than to hear mine. Besides which I wanted to hear him talk.

Djo is simple and truthful. I am complicated and full of doubts. When I think too hard, I act stupidly.

I waited too long.

The doctor gave Djo an injection, and at last he stopped shaking. Now Djo sleeps more and more. The doctor says it is good for him. The doctor does not look me in the eye when he says this. Outside is as hot as ever, but inside I am cold with dread.

I touch Djo's arm, almost accidentally. It makes him shift and breathe suddenly more deeply, as if remembering to be alive. Then he drifts down deep again.

95

Titid has gone to the north, to speak to a farmers' group. He is President now, and always in demand. Still, he came by before he left, to check on Djo.

Titid stood a long time beside the bed, his hand on Djo's arm. I could not tell if he was praying. His hand was shaking a little, vibrating as if he were giving Djo a transfusion of energy.

When Titid turned to me, he took my uniform collar in his two hands. That way, with his fists resting on my collarbones, he looked for a long time straight into my eyes. His own eyes look very big up close, through his thick glasses. I was not uncomfortable.

"My dear," he said, and I knew both that he had forgotten my name and that he knew and loved me. "Take care of Djo, yes?"

I nodded.

"And you, yourself. Get some sleep." With his thumbs he traced circles under my eyes. "Exams are coming up, not so? You will study?"

I moved my head noncommittally, and he smiled.

"Why not record your own story, too, Jeremie?" he asked, suddenly remembering my name.

Only Titid himself could do all these things at once. He must want to keep my mind off worry.

To take care of Djo is all I really want to do. I don't care about the other things. I don't need sleep.

96

If only, if only there were something I could do for Djo. Give blood. Anything. The doctor says no, and that I should just go back to school. But if—*when*—Djo wakes up, I want to be here.

I could study, to pass the time. Titid is right: final examinations are nearing—my last exams. I am almost through high school. For seven years I have been preparing for these exams, and now I can't even think of them. They seem suddenly pointless to me. To please the nuns, I carry a big satchel of books, but there are more pressing things to make sense of.

I want to talk to Djo.

Or at least write. I don't picture him reading . . . but of course he reads, since he taught the boys! I picture him better playing soccer, or dancing.

It was four months ago that I first noticed Djo. It was one of the first days of school. The election campaign had just begun. I was walking on clouds that day, proud to be beginning my Philosophy Year, as the nuns call this last one. My friend Liliane and I were coming home from school, taking the long way, stretching the afternoon. In a far corner of the convent park we heard laughter, and when we looked we saw one tall, strong boy waving a flat stick, and all around him little boys jumping.

"Who is that?" I asked Liliane, who usually knows.

"That is Djo, new man on Titid's election team," said Liliane, squeezing my arm.

I laughed. There was something about this Djo person that made me feel happy. He was knocking mangoes from a tree for the small boys, and every time he hit one they cheered. He swung the stick—*whap!*—and a mango fell into the hands reaching up. I wanted to stay and watch him for a long time.

"Come on, come on," said Liliane. "Walk with me, and I'll tell you all about him."

She didn't know much, just how to lead me away.

"They say he's been away in another country, and now he's back, one of Titid's team."

And what are they to Aristide? I wondered. Bodyguards? Advisers? Comrades? It was mysterious to me and also very impressive.

Titid. I have been hearing about Titid, Father Aristide, and hearing his voice on the radio, for about five years now. When he had a church, I used to go to mass to hear him preach. When he spoke, I felt as if he was inside my head, stretching and stretching it. So hard I had to think, following every word.

Once at mass Liliane whispered to me, "Psst, Jeremie! Shut your mouth. Always in the middle of Titid's sermon your mouth falls open."

Once, leaving mass, I was thinking so hard that I forgot my shoes, which because they were too tight, I had left under my pew.

98

My friends teased me: "She is otherworldly, you know. . . . Our Jeremie has become angel with no thought of body."

And now this same Titid, who spins the puzzling words, who has awakened all Haiti by his speeches and his work, has given me the job of interviewing this same Djo that I have been admiring from afar. I cannot believe how lucky I am.

"Djo may very well die, Jeremie," Titid told me just before he left. "You must look that sadness in the face, every day."

If Djo dies, his story will be part of me. I will be alive.

15

There is a transparent tube that goes from the bag of sugar water that the doctor hung above Djo's head. Down into Djo's arm it goes, into the inside of his arm right above his hand. I watch the sugar water travel down slowly. Sometimes there are bubbles of air, and when they are big, I worry. Could air hurt a person, going inside? Once, when blood came out of Djo's arm into the tube, I got so scared I called the orderly. He came running, his sandals flapping on the concrete floor, but then he said it was all right and not to worry. The tube, called IV, and other supplies for Djo were sent by missionaries after they read in the paper what had happened to Djo and the other boys.

The doctor is sad, and busy all the time. Another boy from Lafanmi has died, a little boy only seven.

In the quiet today I feel Djo drifting away, too. People keep saying, "He is young, and the young heal quickly." But I think, The other boy was younger, and a body can take only so much.

What can I do to pull Djo back? I can rub his feet, and I can talk. There does not seem to be much else. It is strange to become acquainted with someone's feet and never touch the rest of him.

Yesterday Djo wanted me to talk about myself, and I wouldn't. Now I keep thinking of things I want to tell him. Everything, in fact.

Djo's life so far makes a sort of story, but does mine? I have not thought about that until now. When you are in the middle of it, life is one big jumble. You don't think of it as a story.

Well, if I don't yet have a whole story, I do have a life.

When I think about before I started school, what I remember best is making kites. If I write about that, and talk about it out loud to Djo, maybe he will hear, and maybe just the sound of a voice will draw him back. The orderly says that happens sometimes.

My Philosophy notebook already looks to me like a relic from the past. In a few weeks I won't need it anymore. And it is only half-full of notes, tiny and neat. If I turn it upside down and write from the back . . .

Living next to a dump, it is possible for a small girl with determination to find all sorts of kite material: sticks; plastic wrapping; colored paper sometimes; string; pieces of light, light aluminum; shreds of plastic label off pop bottles. Anything that could twist and twirl and flutter I collected in a box and kept under my bed. Maman checked my box for "bad things." She also kept me supplied with glue, which she made of flour and water.

Back then, when I was growing from baby to little girl, I had two white dresses. One to wear and one to wash. Maman kept me scrubbed, with my hair braided so tight it pulled my skin. I learned to jump over the puddles and trash heaps and to avoid rot and mess, to keep my plastic sandals clean. And all the time running, looking up, following my kite or pulling my kite to follow me. I loved the dump, the sky after sunset the color of mango, with light purple coming up like the inside of seashells. All around, low to the ground, the shacks and shanties of La Saline. Soft colors of rusted tin and old boards, twists of smoke rising from cook fires. Way up in the sky, along with the sea gulls, my kite, tugging up and up to catch the last gold flash of sun.

I live with just Maman, and Auntie. Like yours, Djo, my father left long ago, looking for work. "We were married in the church," Maman says. "Your father was a good man, an honorable man." She uses the past tense. She does not expect him back. Maman is ill most of the time, with fevers that come and go. In the throes of fever she is a visionary. I wonder sometimes if she invented my father in a fever dream.

The clues she gives do not add up to a substantial person in my mind.

"Your father wanted you to get a good education" is one clue. So Maman enrolled me in the nuns' school, against Auntie's wishes. Handed me over to the nuns.

"They recognize promise," says Maman.

"They recognize a strong back in a black skin," says Auntie.

Maman admires Sister Claire, my headmistress. Auntie does not. Sister is *blan*. This makes Auntie suspicious. The nuns love me, I know, but it is the kind of love you have to work for all the time. They, especially Sister Claire, have plans for who I will be. The possibility of disappointing them hangs over me.

At least, if I disappoint them, I will please Auntie!

After I started school, Djo, my kite days ended. Maman made our eating table into a study table, with everything neatly in place—notebooks, two pencils, the knife for sharpening, and a candle stuck in a bottle.

"So where can I put my plate now?" I asked Maman.

"Just set it on the altar to Education," said Auntie wickedly.

"No," said Maman, not even noticing, "from now on we will leave the table for your books and things, Jeri. I wish you could have electric light for studying, but is expensive and not so reliable."

She still sent me for water at the pump, but she began doing other things for me, things I could do perfectly well—cooking rice, peeling onions, scrubbing clothes. She pushed me to study instead of helping. She began telling people how smart I was. Auntie pulled the other way.

"Why don't you do something useful like make a kite, Jeremie?" asked Auntie. "Why you always studying some foolishness about French king?"

"Leave my girl be, Sister," Maman broke in. "Is Education and Education alone will free her from this misery we in."

I looked at Auntie sideways, wondering what misery was that.

"You sound like Education be a fatal disease, Sister," said my auntie. "And maybe you right," she added.

I ducked my head down and pretended to study, to be out of the fight.

I began my career of taking prizes at school. Each time this happens, even now, the nuns beam and kiss my cheek and shake my hand and give me fancy certificates that Maman plasters on the cardboard wall at home. She does it with wheat paste, so that Auntie and I can't take the certificates down.

I overheard the nuns talking one day. It made my heart jump to realize they were talking about me. It made my knees shake with embarrassment.

"Only eleven, but so—*tch*—developed. A shame. Such a bright girl. . . . If we give her work, it will keep her busy, keep her off the streets for a while at least."

And soon after, sure enough, they gave me a shift and a mop and released Maman from the debt of school fees.

Ever since then, instead of paying money for school, I clean the tile floors of the nuns' house. They like the floors damp mopped twice a day.

From the very first morning at the nuns' house, my life seemed different to me, Djo. It took a long time to get the work done, that first day, because I had to stop and look at everything until I could understand what it was. In a wooden frame on the wall was a map labeled PORT-AU-PRINCE, CAPITAL CITY OF THE REPUBLIC OF HAITI. The different sections of the town were in different colors, and I could read the names of some big streets. The sea was printed in blue, with pink islands like La Gonave. Between the city and the sea was a wide gray band that looked to be neither land nor sea. It was marked LANDFILL and, in parentheses, LA SALINE. La Saline is where I live! I saw clearly on the map that it is the biggest slum in Port-au-Prince. I saw that La Saline stretches for many kilometers along the sea, built out on dumped refuse.

What I already knew is that in all of La Saline there are no tile floors that can be mopped, and there are no empty spaces. The nuns' house, at the edge of La Saline, felt sturdy and solid, cool and calm. There is space there, and there is nothing extra. Palm trees in pots blow gently in the breeze, and the nuns in their white robes walk so quietly and speak so softly that often the only sound you hear, besides the flopping of my mop, is the soft wooden click of their rosary beads.

They gave me a new school uniform, light blue, the color of sky. The nuns told me it is the color of purity, of virginity. They associate the two. Daily I dust the statue of Mary in her sky blue robe.

I have been wearing it for six years, Djo, and the clean strong cloth of my uniform still pleases me. There is dirt and mud in La Saline, where, as I see now, no one has real houses, only packing crates and hammered-out tins and whatever else will keep a family somewhat dry and private. La Saline-on-Garbage: the air sharp with the smell of rotting oranges, sour with the smell of latrines shared by many. In the rainy season dirty water runs everywhere, and people cough and spit because they must.

The sun makes things pure. We hang our clothes out between the shacks to be bleached in the sun.

I iron my uniform every day, Djo. Yes! I have an iron. Not the kind the nuns have, with an electric cord that plugs into the wall. The kind people have, an iron box in which I put a coal left over from cooking.

At the convent, when I mop, I hang my uniform on a wire hanger in the nuns' closet and slip on my old brown shift, in which I feel comfortable and almost invisible.

With my mop and my rags I spread cleanliness like a blessing all around the nuns' quiet house.

The orderly comes in. I quit writing. My pencil is down to a stub anyway. He starts to mop under my feet.

"Can I help?" I ask him.

"Oh, no, *mamzelle.*" He seems shocked. He is shy of me as I am sometimes shy of Djo. It gives me courage.

"Don't call me *mamzelle*. My name is Jeremie, like the town."

Now he calls me *Mamzelle* Jeremie. What a mouthful! His name is Emilien. He has hurried to find me a knife to sharpen my pencil. I am hoping it is not something surgical.

Once Sister Claire overheard some of the children who live near me in La Saline teasing me about my clean uniform.

"Don't pay them any mind," she said. "They are just ragamuffins."

No, I thought, they are just children who do not have school fees. But I felt superior anyway. To the children because of my uniform, and to Sister Claire because of my understanding.

I'm not nice, Djo. Not very nice.

I first saw Titid's house, his church and his boys, when I was eleven. I had just begun working for the nuns, and Sister Claire had an errand to do at St. Jean Bosco.

"My! This place could use a cleanup," remarked Sister Claire. And she was right. Pe Titid kept guinea fowl in the courtyard. I wrinkled my nose. I hoped she would not ask me to clean *here*!

To make things worse, as Sister Claire explained to me, Father Aristide collected boys who lived on the street—those who beg, wash windows, steal. *Sansmamans*, people call them.

"They have no mother to tell them how to act, so they behave badly," explained Sister Claire. "What do you expect?"

I recognized some of the boys from the alleys of La

Saline. I wondered if Father Aristide knew that his boys sniffed turpentine and that some of them even sold their bodies to foreigners. I wondered if he knew that they slashed tires, cut each other with razors. Surely he saw them fight like dogs over food.

And yet that day, as I stood in the courtyard very clean and neat in my uniform, while Sister Claire talked to the priest Aristide, boys kept running up to Titid, ducking under his legs, holding his arm for a moment, asking him questions. And it seemed that he loved those boys.

"Love and truth are the same," I heard Titid say later, in a sermon. "Truth and love are Jesus in the midst of the poor."

This is the kind of thing Titid says. At one moment it seems natural, easy to understand. "Of course!" you say. And then sometimes the meaning just slips away. You can't grab it.

Maybe, Djo, he means that you can only love somebody if you are willing to see them truthfully.

And to let them see you truthfully? This is hard, for me. I think I will be the last person to know who I am, truthfully.

Why am I writing this to Djo? He sleeps and sleeps. Even when he wakes up, I may not have the nerve to read it to him. And he can't hold the paper. Not yet, anyway.

It is strange to think that Djo was one of those boys. Djo and Lally, Marcel and Fortuné.

I never thought I would want to know any of Father Aristide's boys. I thought they would all be rough and mean. I guess, to be truthful, I thought I was better than them. That was before I met Djo.

16

Liliane has been asking me about Djo.

"How tall is he?"

I don't know. What I remember about him from before is that he was always moving. Now he fills the length of the hospital cot, his ribs visible under the white sheet. And so still.

"Is his face all mashed like they say, Jeri?"

I am getting used to his face. At first I felt sick and couldn't look at his eyes. There is bright red blood in the whites, and the whites are yellow, and all around is bruised and puffy. At first it was hard to look at him and not make a face. It was hard not to cry. His teeth are broken off, both of the front ones. When he smiles, and he does sometimes, in spite of everything, he looks silly and sad both, like a six-year-old who suddenly got too big.

Yes, Liliane. He is ugly now. I don't mind for me, but I mind for him.

I like to talk to Liliane about Djo. And she knows it. Liliane asked yesterday, just out of the blue, as we were walking past the early morning cook fires on our way to school, "What will your maman say, Jeremie, her fine, smart daughter falling in love with a street kid *sansmaman* who will never leave the slums?"

"Liliane, you are crazy!" I said, as soon as I could catch my breath. But she is right, of course.

I LOVE DJO!

I could write that a thousand times.

JEREMIE LOVES DJO.

Tomorrow I will have known him for eight days.

I should throw this page away, burn it maybe.

No, I should be like whoever wrote on the wall, NOU RENMEN DJO. WE LOVE DJO. Whoever wrote that, I love them, too.

Liliane knows me well. She says that I just think I love Djo because he is so hurt. She says this is no time to be sentimental. That Djo and I are too different for things to be good between us if and when he gets well.

But I truly think that what is happening here is something even Liliane can't understand.

So, Djo. It is true that we are different. But as I think about it, I see that a lot of the difference isn't between you and me.

Some of the difference lies in the way we have been growing up.

Only now I see what happened, Djo.

When I was little, Maman looked around, and here is what she saw. She saw that in La Saline the shiniest, healthiest-looking, and best-dressed children go to the church schools. They go to the nuns and priests and they get Education. The brightest of these children stay in school many years. They take prizes, get scholarships. These are the children who work their way out of La Saline. The luckiest and smartest among them, by the time they are grown up, can work their way out of Haiti altogether.

Because she loves me, Maman put me on that ladder, the ladder out of La Saline. Without quite meaning to, without thinking about it exactly, she told me something like this: "Climb, girl. Don't worry about the others. You are better than they are. Just climb!"

So without thinking about it, that is what I have been doing.

And you, Djo, you never imagined or wanted a ladder out. Because of Titid, maybe. And yes, because you never had somebody like my maman dedicating her life to you. If this whole ladder business were ever presented to you at all, you would probably say,

"Since everybody can't leave La Saline, let's stay in La Saline and try to make things better for everybody."

You have never said these things to me in these words, Djo. But do I guess right that that is how you believe?

Liliane is right that Djo will not leave La Saline or places like it, will not leave Haiti.

Isn't she, Djo?

While I mopped and studied and tried to be the Jeremie everyone was proud of, you were washing cars, dodging *taptaps*, defending Lally. Working on your political education, and learning to be a teacher.

While Titid was getting in trouble with the church for speaking out against the dictator who still controlled all the resources of Haiti, the nuns referred to that same fat dictator as President for Life and forbade us to make jokes about him.

People all over Haiti have been waking up. But people like me, those of us who are so busy busy busy climbing our shaky ladders out of the old mess—we are the last to see it.

And everything that has been happening in Haiti—the demonstrations, hunger strikes, the voting and all—they have to do with us, Djo. With how we are and what we can be together.

Even I, with my snooty attitude and my ladder out, I was dragged into events.

It was just after you were kidnapped and taken to the Dominican Republic that the dictator Jean-Claude Duvalier was finally persuaded to leave our Haiti.

Auntie tells me he went to the beach in France.

"He need to work on his suntan," she says, grinning. "Is married too long to that pale, skinny woman. Lose all his blackness."

I heard the nuns talking. It seemed that maybe Titid's sermons had something to do with the dictator finally leaving. Do you know about that?

"Djo, I was twelve when Duvalier left Haiti. It was February 1986. Such dancing and yelling and singing in the street! And all night long the sound of the *lambi*, the conch shell, the sound Auntie says people used back at the time of the slave revolts. The call for change, the call for revolution. To hear it from so many directions, all night long, it sent shivers down my back.

"Just that year people started doing the dance called the *compas bolero*. It is that glued-together dance, you know, Djo: the man puts his elbows on your hipbones. I remember dancing with my nose in somebody's shirt pocket. I didn't like it, Djo, and I haven't danced the *compas bolero* since.

"And what about you, Djo? These are good dancing feet. Will they dance again? We'll make them dance again, Djo.

"I like *merengue*, where you move so fast everything is a blur except for your very own backbone and bottom. You are out there spinning and shaking, sometimes with people clapping and stomping around the sides. In the partying the night Duvalier left, somebody leaned too hard against our house, and a wall fell in. The wall full of certificates! After that, Maman began to worry about me and made me go hide under her bed. I slept under there, and when I woke up the sun was shining, the 'Hallelujah Chorus' was playing on the radio, and people were still dancing."

When I said this, I was watching Djo. His eyes moved under his eyelids, and he seemed to smile a tiny bit. Maybe he hears. . . .

Oh, my. What did I say?

A general took over the presidency. I wonder if you heard about it, Djo, in the Dominican Republic. The general passed a new constitution. It sounded good. The nuns read it to us in school. I only remember where it said the people who had been working for Duvalier, the thieves and thugs and secret police,

116

all those *Macoutes*, could not be in the government anymore.

The other girls in my class and I shook our heads when Sister Claire read us this. We could not believe that a law could be made that would get rid of the *Tonton Macoutes* in a snap of the fingers. To us the *Macoutes* were just like rats, or lightning. A fact of life. We thought Sister Claire was crazy.

"Is only now you notice Sister Claire crazy?" said Auntie, when I relayed the news. "She who think the whole world be run by idea and words on paper?"

We found out that, sure enough, the general was just for show. He put the constitution in a drawer somewhere, up there in the palace. The *Macoutes* still rode around shooting people they didn't like. They even wore the same dark glasses, the same flashy gold chains, the bandannas. They carried the same guns, Uzis mostly. They were always there.

The law did not make them disappear.

Just look what they have done to Djo. What badness, what fear or anger or hunger made them hit Djo so hard, made them kick him on the floor, set fire to his hair?

Titid says that even the *Macoutes* are our brothers. That there is some Cain and some Abel in everyone. But, says Titid, this does not mean we should not resist the evil, both inside us and outside.

When it became obvious that the constitution was not being obeyed, somebody, maybe Titid, maybe someone else, began talking of *dechoukaj*, the word farmers use when they dig up a big stump, one with deep roots. It is a job that takes several men, some crowbars, maybe even chains and a mule. People began using the word *dechoukaj* to talk about getting rid of the *Tonton Macoutes*.

Near school two well-known *Macoutes* in a car gunned down a young man who was writing slogans on a wall. I ran out with some other girls and Sister Claire to see the commotion. A big crowd gathered immediately, people hovering around the dead body.

"Dechouk-le!" someone shouted on the sidewalk, and instead of standing with their mouths open, people spread the shout, ran after the car, caught it in a traffic jam, and dragged out the *Macoutes*. One got away, but the other was beaten by the crowd. *"Dechouk-le!"* they shouted. "We've had enough *Macoutes!"* One man pulled a machete, and soon the *Macoute* was dead, cut to pieces.

"Horrible!" said Sister, white as a sheet.

"He is not more dead than the man he shot," a woman beside her said.

"For a long time, *Macoutes* were being *dechouk*ed, their bodies burned. But there seemed always to be more. It was suicide, Maman said, to be out on the street at night. After dark Maman made me use a chamber pot. I wasn't allowed three steps out the door to go to the latrine.

"And in La Saline we would hear pops of gunshot all through the night. I was glad I shared my bed with Auntie now."

Djo smiled! I am not sure, but I think, I hope, maybe he hears.

Emilien, the orderly, just got up his nerve to send me outside! I am proud of him. I think if I hadn't been talking about using the chamber pot I would not have understood him at all. I am so dumb. Even though Djo is so still, he is alive, and so, like everybody, he needs to pee.

Maybe now Emilien will stop calling me *mamzelle*.

When Emilien finally called me back inside, Djo looked better, propped a little higher on pillows, and with a kind of awareness on his face. He opened his eyes briefly, but only the whites showed, and I was glad when he stopped trying. He held my hand when I touched his. So it is something. I will read what I have written and talk more to him, in case a voice helps. I want to tell him about the elections. I lied to him before. About these hands of mine.

There were elections. Maman said only because the United States wanted them. *Eleksyon pepe-yo*, she called them—secondhand elections. People argued whether to vote.

"I want nothing to do with this foolishness," said Maman.

"As for me, I will grab even this small chance to get a decent man in the palace," said Auntie. "But what do I do when I reach the voting place?"

"You don't have to read, Auntie," I told her. "They will have pictures of the candidates." The nuns had told us this.

"Come with me, Jeremie. Please, Jeri, *cherie*. Then if there are words, you can read them to me."

Well, Djo. I was curious about the whole voting business. Liliane said there would be movie cameras there, foreign journalists taking pictures. I was fourteen, and everywhere I went people whistled and complimented me. I would not mind having my picture taken. So without telling Maman, who would surely say no, I went.

The voting was taking place in a school in the Ruelle Vaillant. What happened there is famous now. Djo, I'm glad you weren't there.

The school at Ruelle Vaillant had open classrooms around a courtyard, the courtyard surrounded by high walls topped with broken glass. Maybe once it was a rich person's house. The election officials sat at a long table with ballots on it, and also big wooden boxes for the votes. There were five stacks of ballots, one for each candidate, printed with the man's name and his picture. People were lined up to vote, dressed up in their best clothes. One lady was all in pink, with a pink straw hat. Sure enough, a white woman was taking her picture. One old man even wore a suit coat. His wedding coat, maybe, so old it was. As he approached the voting table, he held his hat against his chest, respectfully, like a person going into church.

When Auntie got to the front of the line, she told the people she wanted to vote for Met Gourgue. They handed her his picture. She showed it to me, and I nodded. She grinned, folded it neatly, and stuck it into the wooden box.

After Auntie had voted, we went on out the gate of the school. Then a woman I knew, the mother of a friend, came in, and I went back inside the courtyard to greet her. I heard jeeps pull up outside, but I didn't pay attention. Suddenly the woman I was talking to looked up; her face got lopsided, Djo. I looked over my shoulder. Men were coming in with machine guns held in front of them. They started shooting right then. I ran toward the gate, but it was blocked with people screaming and struggling to get out, falling in pain or dead. Already blood covered the ground and painted the wall.

I could not hear myself screaming, Djo, but my throat was on fire. I could not see my aunt anywhere. The gateway was completely blocked, and more bodies were piling up.

The only way out, unbelievably, was over that wall with the broken glass in it. People were going over, too. I could see their legs.

I did not think that I had the strength to pull myself up onto that wall, or the courage to grab those sharp pieces of glass, to use them as handles even as they cut my hands, to drag my stomach and legs across them. But I did it, Djo. The guns and screams behind me did it for me, really. I fell to the other side of the wall. My hands were slick with blood. I couldn't see, just blurs of color. I was terrified of falling into the hands of soldiers.

The other day you felt my hands, Djo. Remember? "Why are they so rough?" you asked. "Do you work so very hard, Jeremie? Do you strip palm at home?" The doctor has told me to say only restful things to you, so I said, "Yes, Djo. Stripping palm is one of my jobs."

Hands that were not soldier hands took hold of me, pulling my torn dress and my torn flesh together. Two women, I think, carried me between them down Grande Rue and into a doorway.

"Why?" I asked Maman, as she cried and bathed me. Auntie was there, too. She said twenty had been killed. She went back to see, and I heard her tell Maman how it was, a desolation of lost shoes and hats, of blood, of burned ballots floating in the breeze, sticking in the blood.

"Why would anybody do it, Maman?"

"Those who hire the *Macoutes* will do anything to stay in power. The general held these sham elections because he thought he could control them. Call Haiti a democracy and keep getting money from the United States. But when Met Gourgue began to win, the general decided to stop them."

"De-mo-cra-cy," said Auntie between her teeth. "What kind of a word is that?"

"Greek," I said automatically. Crying and bleeding, I was still Miss Dictionary. "A country that is run by its people."

"Henh!" said Auntie.

Sure enough, the elections were canceled, "because of violence," the radio said.

The government radio report made it sound as if the violence was caused by us, the people voting. It made it sound as if the people of Haiti were not civilized enough to vote.

But on Radio Soleil, the Catholic radio station, Titid spoke, and he had other things to say.

"To the people who bravely went to vote at Ruelle

Vaillant and everywhere in the country, we take our hats off. We congratulate you on your courage.

"But we must be truthful, too.

"Our cold neighbor to the north wants a democracy in Haiti. Yes, and we the people of Haiti want a democracy in Haiti. But what is a democracy if people are starving? How can you trust a vote when a man will vote for whoever gives him the money to feed his children that night? Starving men will vote in exchange for a plate of rice or a glass of rum or a can of concentrated milk.

"Some men, with guns in their hands and no chance to make an honest living, will shoot their brothers for a few dollars and a bottle of rum. . . ."

I got dizzy, Djo. I think I fainted. I couldn't, couldn't listen to more.

17

"**O**h, Djo. If you are hearing any of this, I hope it is not making you hurt more. I myself am shaking now. Feel my hands, Djo? Your feet feel warm and solid to me. More reliable than my cold shaky hands.

"I did not want to be involved in voting again, Djo, or in the talk about democracy or government or freedom of the people to self-determination. I told myself that it was all just *blablabla*.

"I stayed in bed for a week. Maman and Auntie both fussed over me, boiling water to bathe me, changing bandages, spending coins fished from a hole in the mattress for a chicken to make soup. The nuns sent medicine and even came to pray with me. Maman and Auntie nursed me so well that with all the cuts I didn't even get a fever. My skin healed.

"The nuns were kind to me, with their ointments and bandages and sympathy. They offered me their busy, useful detachment. They offered me peace, Djo."

People say, when someone dies, Well, at least he is at peace. Are you tempted, Djo, just to let go and be at peace? I would understand that. I would be very miserable, though. And angry! Yes. It is a surprise to me, to know that I would be angry with you for choosing death.

I had better not read these last few lines to Djo. Does he need me to fuss at him? Alone and maybe dying here, does he need some girl angry with him?

Still, I believe, and not just because I want to, I believe that if Djo dies, it will not be by choice. And believing that, I find I can't be angry with Djo at all.

So Sister Claire and the other nuns wanted to protect me from the world, Djo. For a while, I welcomed the gift.

When I went back to school and to work, I began preparing to become a nun.

As I covered the clean tile floors with gentle floppings of wet mop, I prayed under my breath for the people who had tried to vote. I said Hail Marys, Our Fathers, remembering my intention by thinking of the old man's hat, held against his chest. That was as close as I could go to thinking about Ruelle Vaillant.

I studied, Djo, and learned about things that happened long ago and far away: the Roman Empire, the crowning of Charlemagne, the siege of Paris. I learned by heart poems written halfway around the world. I mopped the clean floors. I peeled *battata* under the picture of Jesus. I knelt in the chapel every day, holding the smooth, cool rosary beads Sister gave me, playing them one by one through my fingers as I repeated the prayers.

And what was Djo doing then?

Djo had just buried Donay.

"Djo, are you there?" I hold his hand. I touch his face, very lightly. He seems to try to open his eyes. I think he is there, right under the surface. I think he hears me.

I stayed away from Titid's church, from St. Jean Bosco. Titid's words were too disturbing. If love plus truth equals what happened at Ruelle Vaillant, I did not want them, Djo.

127

A year passed. I did my work. I studied. Maybe, like you, Djo, I was in mourning.

Then came my fifteenth birthday. Maman makes a fuss about birthdays. You don't even remember when yours is, do you, Djo? On my fifteenth birthday Liliane brought over a whole jar of hair beads. All morning we sat out on the bench beside the door, plaiting each others' hair in rows and loops, receiving the compliments of passersby and the bunch of admiring small children who gathered around us. I felt like a princess. It seemed the first time since I was a child just to sit in the sun and laugh.

Then Liliane said to me, "Jeremie! We are so beautiful! Let's go to church tomorrow. You used to love it. It is so exciting there. You never know what Pe Titid will say. Please, Jeri, you can wear my sister's shoes!"

Maybe I was through grieving. Maybe I was bored, Djo, and a little lonesome in my life with the nuns. Probably I was just vain. But I agreed to go.

The courtyard of St. Jean Bosco, the steps of the church, were crowded with people. Some were dressed for celebration, some as if for work. One boy sweated in a tank top, his basketball clutched under his arm. (Was it you, Djo, maybe? No. You were still in the Dominican Republic then. For another year you would still be in the D.R.)

128

I sat with Liliane in the high, shady church. I saw the people around me, calm, happy, excited in the way of people open to the spirit.

People began to sing:

"Hallelujah for the Lord in heavens
We will applaud you
We will celebrate you
We will dance for you—"

Suddenly, Djo, my new happiness left. I was not happy anymore, but angry. I thought of the lady dressed in pink, to celebrate the voting. I felt stupid in my hair beads, and I was too angry to sing.

Then Father Aristide, looking small and frail in his white cassock, walked to the pulpit. He looked at us; he greeted us. And then he spoke:

"We do not really merit the grace of God if we refuse to think about the words we sing. 'Hallelujah,' we sing. A word of rejoicing. But in our hearts we mourn. Many of us are thinking, How can we rejoice when our brothers and sisters have been slain at Ruelle Vaillant and at so many other places?"

Once again, Djo, my mouth fell open in wonderment. Had Titid read my mind?

"Instead of singing," he continued, "some of us are asking, 'When, O Father, are we going to live in peace?'

"And our Father responds, 'You will live in peace when you wrap your faith and your commitment together in a people's church that will permit the people's power to come to a boil in a people's revolution—so that this country can breathe free.'

"This is the way the Lord of light speaks to us. If we accept His light, we will rightly say, 'Hallelujah to the Lord in heaven.' We will rightly applaud Him. We will rightly dance for Him."

From that day I went to St. Jean Bosco every time Titid was there to preach. And through Titid I began to understand what I feared so much, why I could not make myself think about the killing at Ruelle Vaillant.

It was like this, Djo. Honor and respect for the people who were killed at Ruelle Vaillant required me to take action, to take risk. After all, Djo, the whole reason those people came out to vote was to make things different. So we owe them something. But remembering what happened to them reminded me how big the risk was. It was too big for me, Djo. I was scared, so very scared. Too scared to be honest, Djo. Too scared to be truthful. At least I was beginning to see this, and to look for a new way to be.

Titid's sermons were mostly questions that summer: he was teaching us to think, Djo. To be less helpless, more hopeful. To face up to the questions of power and responsibility and risk. And you know, we were helping him, too. We fed him love and energy. He fed us ideas and logic. We were in confusion, Djo, the people sitting in the pews at St. Jean Bosco, all kinds of people. There was a big task pressing in on us, a big responsibility: to shoulder some power, to uproot the dictator's thugs, to be effective and thorough without becoming vengeful.

Titid's questions helped us realize that if you are confused, it is because you want to understand. His questions helped us turn our confusion to energy, to action. When I heard his voice in speeches and sermons broadcast all over the country on the Catholic radio station, it seemed that it was as much our voice, our thoughts, as Titid's. They were the same. And not something finished, Djo. Not something already all thought out and decided. Thought was growing from confusion all the time. Pushing and questioning.

At the convent school, I helped the nuns with one last polishing before all the students came back. School had been closed a while, for the break and because the nuns feared violence. There was shooting in the streets, and sometimes schoolchildren had been hit.

"I hope you are staying out of trouble, Jeremie," said Sister Claire, upending a chair to dust the bottom, and looking at me suspiciously.

"A responsible person in Haiti cannot stay far from trouble," I heard myself say.

131

Sister Claire straightened. "You sound as if you have been around Father Aristide," she said. "I think you should be very careful, Jeremie. Father Aristide is far too outspoken. The role of the church is to promote peace, not to incite violence."

My throat went dry. I wanted to tell her that I had changed, and that she should change, too. Would the church promote peace by closing the school? Would we promote peace by closing our eyes and praying to heaven? But I was still too scared, Djo. I just closed my face and slapped my scrubbing rag on a chair leg.

Titid had so many enemies already. Was the church also turning against him?

Of course it was, Djo! You knew that a long time before I noticed. Miss Pass All Examinations was just waking up.

I read this part to Djo with my hand on his foot. His foot is alive, warm, and he moves his toes. I have a hope that he hears.

But Emilien came in again, and I can't read out loud when he is here, even though he wants me to. This story is for Djo, not for Emilien!

So I talked to Emilien, and now he is gone, and I can write again.

Because I was mad with Sister Claire for her narrow views, and with myself for being so cowardly,

132

I decided to go to vespers at St. Jean Bosco. Nights were as dangerous as ever.

Maman didn't allow it.

Sister Claire told me not to.

I made up my mind to go that very night.

The congregation at evening mass looked more tired than on Sunday morning. Maybe it was the end of the hottest season, or the building of a storm, for we were coming into hurricane season, or maybe it was just because most people had worked hard all day. Many people did not have shoes on. The woman in front of me sat stooped, and I knew her back hurt. I wanted to reach out to rub her shoulders, but I was too proper to do it. She had two small boys with her, full of pep. The one would hook the other with his foot, trying to make him fall. The brother would grab the pew back, falling, trying to come down quiet. The mother sighed her weary sigh.

When Titid came in, things took on focus. The murmur among people was more purposeful, like bees in a hive. The woman in front of me sat up straighter. The boys quieted down and watched to see what Titid would do. And what did Titid do? He looked out at people. He smiled. He showed that he, too, was tired, but that he was glad to see everybody. "We are not here to mess around," he said. "Let us pray, and let us mean what we say." Together, we prayed. Familiar words, turning them over for new meanings.

133

After mass Titid said, "Let us sing, with true spirit, meaning what we sing." It was one of the songs that started in Jean Bosco. It is about the things we hope for in a new Haiti, what we were talking about, Djo—

> *"A house with a roof*
> *Water to drink*
> *A good plate of rice and beans*
> *A field to work in—"*

In the middle of the song there was a crash outside so loud no one could ignore it. The voices faltered a little, but seeing that Titid was singing loudly, we kept singing, too. We tried to mean what we said. We tried to sing what we meant. When we finished, and listened again, we understood that someone was throwing rocks against the outside of the church, against the walls of the church. Not just one person, because the crashes were coming from all sides. Many people were throwing rocks. Suddenly a window broke, with a different sound. Glass tinkled down inside the church. I thought of Ruelle Vaillant and dug my fingernails into the scars on my hands, wishing I could become small, immaterial. A shot whined through the air, pinged against the wall; then another and another. The congregation was there, standing, ready to panic but not knowing where to go.

"Friends," said Aristide, in his calmest voice, "do not try to leave. Come closer, and we will sing together, if we can find our true voices."

Djo, we sang and prayed for so long it seemed the whole night—time to find and lose bravery many times. Men outside shouted insults, but mostly we didn't hear them. Once, in a silence, I heard someone shout, "We'll be back Sunday. Don't rest, little priest. We'll be back." When we heard the sounds of Jeeps revving up, we fell on our knees, cheering. Titid offered a prayer of thanks.

Coming out of the church, the people of the congregation hugged one another, touched hands, arms, faces. The woman who had been in front of me— Sylvie—was like my sister now. She hugged me, and I pounded her back where I knew it hurt, while the boys danced around pretending they had machine guns. We were alive and in one piece. Even mostly of one heart, Djo, except for those crazy little boys.

Djo has been asleep a day and night. The doctor and Emilien call it a coma. I hold my breath to hear Djo breathe.

And still I believe that he is there, that he can hear my voice. That he is gathering strength somewhere deep inside.

18

Back home, late in the night, Maman had just about given me up for dead. She was too sick with worry to notice I was safe. Even when I told everything that had happened, I was not forgiven. This time not even Auntie sided with me.

"Your Maman has enough problem, enough sorrow. And you her onliest child. Is not right to make her worry so. You big now, Jeremie, for true, but you not have the judgment for the thing you get involved in. You not got experience, you know."

I wondered, Does anybody in all Haiti have experience to guide them in the situation we are in now? Does anybody have experience to build the decent poor man's life?

"Anyway," said Auntie, "you stay out late one more time, it be your fault or no, and your auntie go whip you from here to Cap Haitien."

I am fifteen years old, I thought. Too old to be threatened so. Too old to be thrashed.

Then it was hurricane season for sure. The air was heavy, and the breeze from the sea didn't come, didn't come. Everybody waiting for air.

"Agwe is holding his breath," people said. "Pulling in his breath for a tremendous blow."

Maman was sick with headaches. She swung her legs over the edge of her cot and sat staring into space, gathering strength to stand up. Her eyes had bruises under them, and her face was shiny with sweat, early in the morning and all through the day. Everything heavy and still, and in the evening the sky was green.

Auntie came in, bringing a story. "So picture this, Sister," she said to Maman. "The little boy is sitting on a crate, fishing in shallow water, nothing but a string on his cane. Suddenly he's on his feet, yelling like a *loa* mount him. And the crowd come. What do they see? Sister, they see the Lully shark, the one that came to warn before the hurricane David. Big and black in the water, pulling and thrashing with nothing to pull against, just that child's little string in his jaw."

Maman stared at Auntie, shaking her head slowly. I could see the gooseflesh come up on her arms, hot as it was.

"But the shark, you know, he act like he hooked. He weave back and forth, back and forth. Every time that fish pass in the water, his eye on the side of

137

his head come up out of the water and stare at the people."

Maman shook herself, and Auntie shrugged.

"You can be sure all those fishermen are dragging their boats up to safety now," she said, with satisfaction. "They moving, let me tell you."

I couldn't stand it.

"Oh, Auntie!" I said to her. "How can a fish know anything?"

Auntie turned on me. "And you, Miss Smartie, Miss Pass All Examinations, how do you think a fish *not* feel the wrath of Agwe? Agwe is spirit of the sea, and when Agwe gets angry, everybody in the sea feel it!"

I felt a shock, Djo. The truth of Auntie's words hit me like a truck.

"*Lavalas* is coming," said Maman, her face glistening. "*Lavalas* the Flood is coming to wash away the wicked."

"Wash away the poor first," said Auntie, practical now. "La Saline be the first to go. Nothing but loose trash and cardboard between us and the sea."

Maman sank down on the chair. She closed her eyes and tilted her head back, stuck her feet straight out, apart. She heaved a big sigh.

"Damballah, Damballah," she said, "send down your cleansing rain."

Eh, Djo. Your mama, too, talked about Damballah. The strong spirit, good and bad together, Damballah the serpent, Damballah the rainbow.

"Let it rain, Damballah," said Maman again, quietly, like a person only rain can save. I went and got a wet rag to put on her forehead.

Auntie was washing beans now, sifting them through her fingers in a pan of water.

"*Lavalas*, wash us like beans. Help us find the wicked and throw them out." She scooped the rotten beans off the surface where they floated, and pitched them out the door.

Djo has been unconscious for two whole days. The sugar water in the IV tube hardly moves. He is thinner: his ribs are like a washboard under the sheet.

Prayer isn't enough. Prayer by itself is nothing.

19

"*Se Lavalas!* Let the Flood descend!"

Father Aristide was at his most passionate—preaching, pleading, celebrating. I could only listen at the radio: it was just four days after the rock throwing at St. Jean Bosco. Maman and Auntie had kept me home from mass and were sitting on either side of me like jailers. All in a row we sat, on our cot, listening to Titid's broadcast sermon on Radio Soleil. His voice was tinny on the radio, but the strength came through.

"Alone, we are weak.
Together, we are strong.
Together, we are the flood."

I looked at Auntie. She was nodding her head in intense agreement, eyes closed. "Amen," she said at intervals.

"Let the flood descend, the flood of
Poor peasants and poor soldiers,
The flood of the poor jobless multitudes. . . .
Let that flood descend!"

"How?" asked Maman, under her breath.

Too restless to sit still with Titid's voice ringing in my ears, I stood and walked to our door. There are no windows in our house, Djo, so the door is always ajar. Maman and Auntie each held out a hand as if to stop me.

"I promise." It was all I needed to say.

"Arise! Go forth! Walk!" shouted Titid on the radio, quoting Scripture again.

"Arise and go forth so that the *Tonton Macoutes* will stop walking in ways wet with our blood.

"Arise and go forth so that the criminals will stop walking upon us.

"Arise and go forth so that the assassins will stop waking us in our beds with rounds of gunfire."

It came back to me very clearly, Djo, how I slipped in blood at Ruelle Vaillant, getting to the wall. This speech was not *blablabla*. What Titid spoke of was entirely real.

I looked out into the bright, bright day. Outside the door a tiny breeze lifted the dust. It carried a

141

rumble, a sound, a chant. At first I paid no mind, Djo, and then I began to hear words:

"Jodi-a se jou male! Jodi-a se jou male!" The chant was repeated over and over, accompanied by sounds of metal against metal.

"Today is a bad day," they were saying. But who were they? The voices were men's voices. The men were marching, prowling, feeding themselves courage for an attack. Past the end of the alley I saw them go, ten, twenty, maybe fifty. Some had on army pants. They carried machetes, knives, spears, and guns. They carried plastic jugs: kerosene? They wore red armbands. They were headed toward the church.

Suddenly, I knew exactly what they would do there, Djo. In my mind I saw them cutting, spearing, shooting Sylvie, her boys, the young and old of the congregation. Titid.

"Maman, Auntie!" I dragged them to the door. "Let me go warn Father Aristide. Bless me, Maman. Let me go."

And in the background Titid's voice, saying, "Arise, go forth."

Maman stood close to me. I saw the sweat in rings under her eyes. She reached up and with her thumb made a cross on my forehead. "Go," she said, giving my shoulder a push. I loved her then, and I thought I would never see her again.

"Go to a phone," said Auntie. "You will never get around them in time." It was a hard decision, Djo, and must be made fast. The only phone nearby was in the other direction from the church, up at Ma Paulie's store. "Go to Ma Paulie," said Auntie.

I ran to Ma Paulie's as fast as I could. My sandals slipped, and I kicked them off to splash without slipping through sewage water, to run faster. A man was using the phone, but just seeing my face, Ma Paulie grabbed it from him, jiggled the receiver holder, and handed it over. The number of the church was familiar to me, and yet for a moment my mind was blank. Then I dialed. I heard the phone ringing, ringing. Everyone there would be listening to Titid's sermon. I pictured the phone, in the sacristy, only a few meters from the nave. So many people must hear it. Please, God, please, please make someone answer. And then I heard a sound like the phone knocked over. Through the wire I heard gunfire, screams, shouts, then a big crack sound, and the phone went dead. And I knew I was too late.

Next thing I remember, Djo, are Ma Paulic's big arms around me, her soft big bosom. And she was rocking me saying, "Is all right, *ma cherie*, is all right, is all right, is all right." And I am saying, "No no no no no, is not all right at all, is not all right." Like a little argument we kept up to keep us from thinking too much. And at last, when I could stand again, she said, "Let me take you home to your maman, before she die of worry," and I let her lead me like a little sheep, and I went home.

On the radio, no news. Radio Soleil was off the air. Black smoke rising up on one side of La Saline, the side where St. Jean Bosco stands. Did stand. The news was all of the hurricane.

It hit that night, ripping off the roofs in La Saline, sending people to shelter as they could with one another, soaked to the bone and dodging pieces of flying tin and debris. The rain, the cold clean rain, falling hard as rocks.

The next day, news at last, through rumor. Many people killed. St. Jean Bosco burned to the ground. Titid alive, once again by miracle—alive, but badly shattered, and in hiding. Each killer, everybody said, was paid a bottle of rum and seven dollars. The bonus, for the one who killed Titid, no one collected.

I am amazed at what I have written here, my hand shaking more and more. Titid was right: I have a story, too, Djo. Another part of our story. And that was two years ago. So much has happened since.

But I will lose heart for the telling if you don't wake up, Djo.

Sister Claire came to the clinic! The doctor sent for her to get her to make me leave.

144

And I argued, I stood up to her. I told her if she wanted to help, she could lend a cot for me to sleep on in the clinic. And then, in the commotion, Djo groaned, moved, opened an eye!

Oh, Sister Claire, thank you. I love your sharp, stern voice, since it woke Djo up!

20

"D jo!"

"Who . . ."

"Who what, Djo? Don't try to talk. Wait! Let me get you some water or something. . . . There. Now, what are you saying?"

"Who the loud lady?"

His voice is a croak, but he is entirely awake, and I can understand him.

"Is Sister Claire, Djo!"

"Well, go outside and talk with your Sister Claire, and then come back in."

"Okay, Djo. Bye, Djo."

So I run out after Sister Claire and catch her in front of the clinic.

"I thank you for coming, Sister."

Sister Claire kisses me on the cheek. Then she stands still holding my hand, looking at me with blue eyes, searching my face for something.

"Your visit helped Djo, Sister," I say. "It helped me, too."

Sister Claire takes a deep breath. "I have good news for you, Jeremie. On condition, of course, that you do well on your examinations, which we are all confident you will."

I feel lost, waiting for her to finish, wanting only to get back to Djo.

"Yes, Sister?"

"I have your mother's assent, of course. I had to get that before the application was sent."

"Application?"

"That is the surprise, my dear!" Sister Claire puts her cool hand on my cheek. "We applied for a university grant. I just got word: there is a place for you at the University of Paris. Yes, my dear, at the Sorbonne!"

"Who, me?" I ask, and laugh, because I am beginning to sound like Djo already. I have to drag my mind back to Sister Claire and her surprise.

"Oh, Sister," I say, feeling as if I am calling from far away. "You have been good to me. Generous and—wise. But I want to stay here, Sister. This will be a good year to be in Haiti."

Sister Claire is silent. She takes a breath as if to say something, and then shakes her head instead.

"Is it because of that boy?" she asks at last.

I nod. Because of what that boy has made me see. And because of that boy.

"Then perhaps we can defer the scholarship."

Until he dies? Until I come to my senses? Her words feel terrible, like punches to the stomach, to the heart.

But she means to be kind. She doesn't understand. She means to be kind.

We talk a while longer, making peace with trivialities. The sun sets red, and bats swoop after mosquitoes. We say good-bye, and at last I watch Sister Claire's determined white form disappear into the dusk. I can go inside!

Emilien has been helping Djo. He is propped higher, on clean sheets, and the IV is gone. Emilien has fed him a little soup. Emilien darts away like a rat when I come in, before I can stop him.

My throat aches, and I don't know what to say.

"You've been far, Djo."

He nods.

"Good to see you, Jeremie." He clears his throat.

This is not easy for him either. I see tears at the corners of his eyes. The best thing seems to be to wipe them away with my hand.

He starts talking, so low I can hardly hear.

"The place where I was, Jeremie, it was all right, you know. It have a pull, most like warmth of sun. . . ." He hesitates, as if he wants to say something else. "But you, Jeri, you be here."

I still can't think what to say. It is as bad as the first day. I begin to shake.

"You not have question to ask me tonight, Jeri?"

I seize the straw.

"Will you talk to me, then, Djo?"

"We have time, you know, Jeremie."

A lifetime, I think. If we continue very, very lucky.

"I mean this tape for Titid, Djo."

"Okay," he says. "Be glad to, Jeremie. But only if you go home and get some sleep first."

III · DJO

21

I did hate to send Jeremie back home. But she look so tired, so tired. The orderly told me how she would not go home for three whole days. How the doctor try to make her go and she look at him high and mighty and refuse flat. That doctor is no match for Jeremie.

"Can't but one person boss a woman in love," the orderly say. I look at him fierce so he not begin to laugh at Jeremie, but now he gone I can't stop smiling.

The orderly Emilien tell me, too, how Jeremie write almost a whole entire book while I lie here like a dead fish. And how she did read it aloud to me, day after day, and talk to me, all because Emilien told her that her voice might bring me back.

❁ I am ready now to finish up this tape-recording business and pick up with life. The healing will be slow, but the doctor says I have chance now. He the most downcast, hopeless fellow, so if he say I have chance I do believe him. Besides, I know I have good chance because Jeremie will be here. Each time I wake up, I think is something good out there. But what? I lie waiting to remember. Then—*ping!*—like a present, like a good song, I remember Jeremie.

So through the long night, let me plan what I will tell her. To finish this part of the story. So we can begin another.

❁ Noon already! The sun high, the lizard soaking in heat, and still no Jeri! Emilien come in and roll me right over. Give me a bath with warm water. Try to make me talk about Jeremie. "You tell the girl sleep, she sleep, man!"

He set about drumming on my back and shoulders, on my legs. "Doctor say we needs to get some circulation." Is all right with me, but it hurt like hell.

Then we hear footsteps. Emilien roll me over, cover me up quick.

"Djo! Emilien! I can come in?"

I feel like I just ran up a mountain. Emilien disappear around one side of the curtain while Jeremie come in the other.

Jeremie come straight to me and give me a kiss. I want to grab her, but I too slow. Before I get my arms up, she sitting on her chair, smiling at me like she the happiest person in the world.

"Djo," she say, shaking her head in wonderment.

And then: "Are you ready to finish the tape, Djo?" at the same time as I say, "So you sleep well, my Jeri?"

I don't want to leave this room just now, even in thought. So I tell her, "Jeri, I don't want to go back to that old story. Let's just go on with today."

"Djo," she says, in a voice that is going to correct me. "You know that old story is part of today. And is our job to get it down. And also I want to hear it. And more than to hear it, you know, Djo. To live it with you."

Jeremie is saying these things and she is not shaking.

❀ "We left me where, Jeri?"

"In the Central Gloria, Dominican Republic."

"Okay, then. For three harvests I swing machete. Three years that be like a lifetime to me.

"Something change in me, Jeri, once I set my mind to stay working at La Gloria, once I did decide to pay for Donay's coffin. Suddenly I want not to see the bad in La Gloria. Is like I want to believe that since this thing that control my life be so big, it must also be good.

"I disappoint Julio by staying. I see it in the way he walk past me and not meet my eye. Julio does not like me anymore. And for my part, I do not admire his restlessness as I did before. Soon Julio leaves without even saying good-bye to me, gone to another work."

✤   The other guards treat me better than before. Allow me even to keep candle and matches, things like that. Remember, Jeri, I tell you how I be a *kongo* donkey to them? Well, is still true, but now I be their favorite *kongo* donkey.

By the time of my third *zafra* I am an old hand already. They make me a cutter and assign to my team a new boy from Jean-Rabel, in north of Haiti. This country boy, name of Roro, is angry, silent, very close faced.

Later, as we work, I try to tell him things not so bad, not so absolutely bad.

This Roro spit and cuss and say nothing. But Roro know how to use machete like it be a piece of his own arm. He very quick and easy to cut cane. The skill I gain in two years he have already when he come in. For that alone I glad the *central* boss give me Roro for a teammate.

Then Roro begin to tell me what been happening in Jean-Rabel, where he come from.

From what Roro tells me, the peasants been meeting in the church to discuss what the laws be about the use of land. If there be some land not in use, then the peasants been grouping together to try to occupy that land. To grow food on it, see, Jeri.

156

"Is a practical thing, Djo," says Roro, "so that people have work and nobody starve. It so practical, we have to fight hard for it. Meet secretly in people house at night, just by small *baleine* light, to learn the law, to discuss the plan."

Roro's words, talking of Jean-Rabel, wake up the teacher Djo in me that been dead three years. I remember at Lafanmi, Titid and Pe Pierre discussing these things.

"You know, Roro, I used to hear about this some. I think this is same organization Titid work with, that he call cooperative."

Roro look so surprised.

"Yes! That is what they do call it. How do you know Titid?"

So I tell him my story, and he look at me like I tell him I the king of France.

"How long you been at La Gloria, Djo?"

"Three years."

"And you not know what been happening all this time in Haiti?" he ask me.

And in truth, Jeremie, I know nothing. So Roro tell me how the people of Jean-Rabel organize and get land to work, but then the big landowners, who never set foot on the place, much less pick up hoe, they call the military, and in they come with gun and machete and kill two hundred peasants, among them be Roro's own father.

So now I know why he be so close faced.

Then he tell me how Titid's church been burned to

157

the ground. I cannot believe it: St. Jean Bosco gone! And he tell me how Titid himself is kicked out of his Order in the church, because they say he been too political. And I remember how Titid say his Order be like family to him. And I was family, too, and did leave him.

"So, Roro, how can he preach if he not have a church?"

"Well, he can't preach so very much now, but he makes speeches instead, and he be on the radio, too—"

And just then the *central* boss come by on a horse, a pistol at his side, and yell at us, "You think you paid to stand jabbering like monkeys? Is to work you are here! Is not garden party!"

He think he so funny. And in fact we is paid exactly nothing anyway.

When he gone, Roro come back close to me, and he have a light in his eye for the first time since I see him.

"Djo," he say. "We go find a radio in this place. We go see what your Titid up to now."

✤ Two days later one of the workers, fellow named Jacot, suddenly fall over dead from heatstroke. He have his bunch of friends, and they take up collection in the evening to buy him coffin like for Donay. They ask me to come play drum at the wake. Is only my second funeral there, and I am thinking about Donay again as they bring in the coffin and put it down in middle of the floor. People all around praying and singing. My eyes noticing the coffin, the handle, the screws. And suddenly, Jeremie, is like cold water go down my back. The screws to the handle not match up. There be dents and scratches. And I see is exactly the same coffin I buy for Donay.

I see how, once again, Donay been cheated, been tricked even when dead, how his old body been dumped with no respect in some hole with lime poured over like for latrine.

And this knowledge is so big, and so bad, that I cannot even think what to do with it.

The next night me and Roro run low through the cane in the moonlight. We come to the small house of one of the *viejos*. This old Haitian man has been at the *central* all his life, and because of this he been given a watchman job at the *central*. He welcomes us a little fearful. He not want anyone to see us come in. Once we are inside, he pats our shoulders; he offers us water from little glass jars and invite us to sit on his cot. And he show us his radio.

"Tonight," he says, "Jean-Bertrand Aristide will speak." There is affection in his voice, and respect. He turns the knob, and is unbelievable but, after some squawky music, Titid's voice comes over.

Titid is talking about the repression in Haiti. He is talking of generals I don't know, of bishops I not quite remember, of things that happened when I was not there. Yet still, Jeri, there is something in his talk that is for me.

"If we live by its rules, we will certainly perish beneath its whip," says Titid's voice. I don't know for sure what he talking about, but I think it does include Central Gloria.

"Disobey the rules. Ask for more. Organize with your brothers and sisters. Keep hope alive," says Titid on the radio.

The old *viejo* look at me with deep smile that night. "You know," he says, "your Titid run for President."

Is my turn for the bug-eye.

"President of what?"

"President of the Republic of Haiti."

❧

Roro and I sit on cut cane, in the shade of uncut cane, chewing on cane. Is breaktime.

"Two things we can do, Roro.

"One, we make a break at night, then follow the ditch up-country. We return to Haiti best way we can and we help Titid win this election."

"Is the only best thing to do, Djo," says Roro, his eyes shining now.

"There be something else, Roro," I say. "When I first come here, I have a good friend, one Donay."

I tell Roro about Donay, how we planned escape, about Donay's death and the coffin.

"And Roro," I say, "that be the same coffin they use again for Jacot."

Roro spit on the cane and say some fine cuss word.

"So the *colmado*-man owe you big money, Djo."

"I think I put my name by one three with five zeroes. I think it be something like three hundred thousand pesos."

Roro whistle.

"I think it be a lot less for rental coffin, Djo!"

Suddenly we laughing.

"I don't owe the man money!" I say.

"He owe *you* money, Djo!"

"If we get the money, we can take bus to Haiti!"

"But how we get it?"

Roro and I, we both sit and think hard.

After a while, Roro look at me right seriously.

"Tonight, we go break into the *colmado* and take back you money. If the *colmado*-man try to stop us— *whap!*—I got sharp machete and I strong. Let he head roll like soccer ball!"

"Lagurie keep what he call a *lengua de Mimi*. You know is machete shaved down thin and sharp. He say it kill a man between the ribs, fast and silent."

We sit thinking.

"Roro."

"Yes."

"Was for Donay I buy the coffin."

"Yes?"

"So the thing to do, for Donay, is the more peaceful thing. The more proud thing. Not to let them make us into thieves or killers."

"You want just only to be his legs, Djo, like the man say."

"I think so, Roro."

"Then tonight we go, the way you and Donay did plan."

"Tonight."

22

"And did it work, Djo? Did the plan succeed?"

"Yes, my Jeremie."

"You make it sound easy, you grinnin' so."

"Not so easy. It was dangerous, Jeri, and the hardest part was to be calm. It was so fun to be smart! Not to play the donkey ever again. It went to our head like strong drink, like *clairin*, but better, Jeri. To be out of the cane. Whooo! You should have seen us trying to walk down the road. Trying not to fly, Jeri, trying not to dance. . . ."

"So tell me, Djo."

❧

Roro says, "Walk in a confident way, Djo. But dignified, man. Imagine you the king of the world, and nobody going to suspect you."

Roro very smart. He show me a clipboard and pen that he had lifted from the tally-man at the *central.*

"When any person stop us, we tell them we been sent by bigwig to count the peoples that live along the ditch."

I still have the old cap Julio gave Donay. It look very good on Roro, with his clipboard.

❀

   "And were people fooled? Did they believe you?"

   "You see me, don't you, Jeremie?"

❀

   There was one place though, up in the mountains. We had decided to leave the ditch and cut straight across to Haiti. Some very high mountains in those part, but beautiful, you know, Jeri. All cut across with little footpaths, steep, but wide enough for a person or burro. And good little farms. Roro say, Oh! If he had land like that! Was like he wanted to kiss it. People growing small plot of cane, or coffee, and things like tomato and onions. Fruit trees, so pretty, lemons, limes. Little plants of *guandule* beans. It look like a good place to live. The houses be of wood sticks with banana-leaf roof or sometimes palm thatch, each so pretty with clay floor and wall the breeze blow right through. So many people have pig, have goat or cow. I think, Oh, this is the decent poor man's life that Titid dream of. This is heaven on earth—a place to work hard and live.

164

We try not to be seen. Is hard, but we travel by night. The paths are narrow and steep, with rocks that roll underfoot. And if you do meet somebody in darkness, they more frightened.

One night, up in the mountain, the moon not up. Only thing I can see is Roro's T-shirt, which in daylight be yellow. So I walking along, eyes glued to the T-shirt, feeling my way, trying not to break my fool neck. Roro, in the lead, stops so sudden I bump right into him. I look up, and right above us be the angle of somebody roof. We inside they house, Jeri!

A voice say, "*Quien está?*" all scared and wavery, you know.

Then Roro make a noise so exactly like a cow! I think, Was a cow I was following? Where is Roro? Till he grab me by the shirt and we scramble across a field and a fence, and I hear a woman calling back behind us, "Juan Blanco, the cow's out!" And Roro bellow out one last moo and 'most give us away laughing.

❀ By day, early, early morning, we come to a river, very cold and fast. Not so deep, it turn out. We feeling our way across with our toes in gravel. Something I been seeing, thinking it was a gray snag of something caught in a branch in the water, suddenly stand up and speak! Roro go under and drink half the river.

"*Buenos dias, Abuela,*" I say in my best Spanish,

for is surely somebody's grandmother, or else maybe a witch or water spirit. I see Roro wading off low, with only his eyes sticking out.

The woman rise up out of the water tall, tall. And very thin like a stick, with old black swimsuit just wrinkly like long skinny legs and long, long gray hair. She at least one hundred years old. But she have teeth, Jeri! Strong old teeth, eyes like gold honey, and she give me suddenly a smile like sun coming up.

"*Rio,*" I say, pointing at river.

"*Rio,*" she say.

"*Haitiano?*" she say.

"*Si,*" I say.

"*Hambre?*" she say. Hungry?

"*Si!*" I say.

Wait, she say with hand gesture. I make the same sign to Roro. The woman take her long hair, she wring it like cloth to take out water, she roll it up neat and tie it in a knot at the back of her neck. She wade to shore and go behind bush. Come out in cotton dress. Now she look ready to go to church. For true she be somebody's grandmother. Great-grandmother, Jeri! She motion us to follow and each to carry a jug of river water. She climb the path as easy as a goat and bring us to her little farm.

The sun shine into her house in stripes through the walls. She have a stove made of the river clay, and a fire of sticks going already. Stew is cooking, goat meat and *guandule* beans. She dish us each a bowl and pour us each cold river water.

166

All day we work quietly on her farm, doing the same things she do. Grind coffee beans in the mortar. Haul water from river. Roro know how to fix the goat pen. Cut and put out fruit to dry in sun. Peel garlic. Shell beans. A few things be hard for her to do alone. Like the house sag a little on one side, so we lift and prop with stone. And we haul clean clay from the river to spread on the kitchen floor.

In the evening, she ask, *"Van por Haiti?"*

"Si. Por Haiti."

She explain the way. Is not far, one day walk only. But she say is better to cross border quietly, by night.

"Hay que dormir," she says, closing her eyes and resting her face on her hand. She shows us to a rope bed. A bed, Jeremie!

Early, early, she wakes us, hands us food, shoos us out.

"Vayan!" she says. *"Vayan con Dios!"*

Roro says nothing. We climb straight up the mountain. Later, we are sitting on a rock looking back down to the river, eating the food she pack for us. Roro take the bone of goat rib he been chewing on. He wave it above the valley and the river, over the beautiful Dominicanie that roll away as far as we can see. He wave the bone something like a priest giving blessing, Jeri. I think is a blessing or salute, for the old lady.

23

"Why you smilin' so, Jeremie?"

"I'm watching your hands, Djo. This is the first time I see you talking with your hands."

"You see the goat rib?"

"I do, Djo. . . . So you and Roro made it back to Port-au-Prince, to Titid?"

"Yes, Jeremie, *m'amie*. And is strange to me that you and I not meet before. For a few months, though, I was not much in the city. I was working on Titid's election up north, with Roro."

"What kind of work, Djo?"

"Explaining to people that never get a chance to vote what election be. That election not necessarily be the same as trick or massacre. . . . My brother Lachaud join up and help out, too. Turn out Lachaud had struck up acquaintance with Titid after I left.

168

Lachaud had come to know the area up north, since he been living a year in Cap Haitien with Mama. Still no word of our father. Roro thinks maybe he died at Jean-Rabel also. . . . I think it possible: so many did die, and many of them men come in for the temporary harvest work."

❀ "And you, Jeremie, you were here in Port-au-Prince, not so? Answering telephone for Titid, Emilien tell me. Taking messages, whether threat or compliment."

"Also, Djo, I was in school. . . ."

Jeremie looks at me as if I suddenly very strange. She puts her hand on top of the fat notebook that Emilien say she fill with words for me.

"Djo," she ask in a small voice. "Do you remember hearing any of my story, that I told you all these days?"

I search my mind. Not much there. "I do remember a little girl in a white dress. I think she was flying a kite?"

Jeremie looks at me. "That's all?"

I can't think of another thing.

Jeremie leans back in her straight chair and tilts her face up to the ceiling, her eyes shut. When she looks back at me, her eyes be full of tears, but she smiling through.

"You've got a lot to read, Djo."

I hold out my hand for the notebook, but she shakes her head.

"I'll leave it right here for you, Djo. This is for you. But today we finish the tape for Titid."

❀

It was only just before the election Titid ask why don't I come back to Port-au-Prince and be with the other boys from Lafanmi Selavi. We be together his bodyguard and team.

And I come, Jeri. Marcel, Lally, Fortuné and me, we have our own room, and we look out for the small boys that live in the shelter.

❀

We look out for them, but not well enough, Jeremie.

❀

When Titid win the election to become President of the Republic of Haiti, is a celebration different from any ever. People rejoice like Easter. People in the streets waving branches, singing. People praying, hoping, frightened, too, because suddenly is our own responsibility, to make a decent life in Haiti.

So when the celebration take place, Titid send all his team and children on the streets to mix in. When a person start to beg from foreigner, we try and say to him, "In the new Haiti, we do not beg."

When a person go start fight, or to cut up some *Macoute*, we say, "In the new Haiti, we settle arguments in the court of law." This be one big teaching job, Jeremie, because is new habit must be made, and also must be made to work.

But the feeling is good, Jeri, don't you think? The air so full of hope is almost fearful. In every speech Titid does congratulate and encourage the young of Haiti.

Inauguration nearing. Titid will become President for true. Three nights before the ceremony, some *Macoutes* pull themselves together, like dying snake, to strike.

They angry at Titid. They want to hurt him. They never can kill him, so they go after his boys.

❀

They sneak into Lafanmi Selavi.

They pour the gasoline.

They light the match.

The boys, asleep on cots and floor mats, catch fire, wake up screaming.

The *Macoutes* throw their stuff around, their little boxes with keys. Big men, bandannas tied around the muscle in their arm, they pocket the boys' car-shine money.

Marcel, Lally, Fortuné and me, we wake up sudden and all at once. Already the smoke enough to choke us, to make the eyes sting so we not see and we run into one another. We know the men are in there. We grab at shadows, and they have fingers to gouge, boots to stomp our bare feet. I grab and bite and fight hard, only knowing by feel and by smell where the enemy is. And when I feel the boots, I glad to know for sure is not one of us I squeeze the breath from. I wish for light. And then one of the roof poles catch fire and I sorry for light. The first thing I see is a small new boy, thrown up against the wall, broken and dead. The next thing, a knife raised, flashing.

"Marcel!" I yell. "Get them out!" Meaning the rest of the boys.

The knife slash down across my face. A small boy runs toward me, grabs the *Macoute* by the leg, hangs on like a guard dog. I proud for him. But another *Macoute* kicks him away, boots him across the floor. I see another machete raised to strike the boy. I see Lally go down, covering the small boy with his body, and the dark blood flow where the machete come down again and again. Others kicking Lally's head. Is then the roof come crashing down. The hot tin doing its damage, yes, but chasing away the killers, too.

"Is hope they want to kill, Jeremie."

"Is hope we need to keep alive, then, Djo."

"And we will, Jeri, don't you think?"

EPILOGUE

We have come from far away in order to arrive
at a remote destination.

We have left the ravine of death in order to arrive
at the top of the mountain of life.

Are we there yet?

No.

Do we want to get there?

Yes.

Can we get there?

Yes.

—From a sermon by Jean-Bertrand Aristide

GLOSSARY

Agwe In the Vaudoun (Voodoo) religion, the spirit of water and the sea.

Aristide, Jean-Bertrand The first democratically elected president of Haiti, Aristide is a Salesian priest whose first and continuing ministry has been among the poor of Port-au-Prince. In this book he is often referred to as Titid, or Pe Titid.

baca Spanish for a spirit monster that takes the form of different animals, from Dominican folklore.

bamboche Creole for a celebration party.

baleine French for whale; Creole for little lamps that used to burn whale oil and now burn kerosene.

battata A Caribbean root vegetable something like a purple potato.

batey An isolated settlement where cane workers live.

blablabla Creole for useless talk, particularly the talk of politicians and government officials.

blan Creole for white.

bracero Spanish for a cane cutter.

Cap Haitien A port city in the north of Haiti.

central Spanish for a sugarcane plantation and processing plant.

charette Creole for a cart with large wheels used to carry cane from the fields to the processing plant.

Cité Soleil A large and very poor section of Port-au-Prince.

clairin Strong Haitian rum.

colmado Spanish for a small store that sells rum and food staples.

compas bolero A dance.

Damballah In the Vaudoun (Voodoo) religion, a unifying spirit of being.

dechoukaj A Creole word used by farmers for the pulling out of deeply rooted stumps. Used politically to mean the process of getting rid of the *Tonton Macoutes*.

Delmas A section of Port-au-Prince.

Dessalines, Jean-Jacques A Haitian general who, with Toussaint L'Ouverture, led the slave rebellion that defeated Napoleon's armies.

Dieudonné A Haitian name that means God-given; Donay's full name in this book.

Dominican Republic A Spanish-speaking Caribbean country that shares the island of Hispaniola with Haiti. The eastern two-thirds of the island are Dominican, the western third Haitian.

Duvalier François Duvalier was dictator of Haiti for fourteen years, and maintained himself in power through a ruthless private army, the *Tonton Macoutes*. In 1971 he died and was succeeded by his son, Jean-Claude Duvalier, who was named President for Life. Jean-Claude Duvalier was deposed in 1986 and now lives in exile.

eleksyon pepe-yo Creole for secondhand, or rigged, elections.

guandule (sometimes **gandule**)   A pigeon pea.

Guinée   Guinea; also used in Haiti to refer to Africa as home-
  land.

ingenio   Spanish for factory or for a sugar processing plant.

Jacmel   A city in southern Haiti.

Jean-Rabel   A town and area in the north of Haiti, the center
  of the peasant-led agricultural reform movement.

Jeremie   A town at the westernmost edge of Haiti, on the sea,
  center of resistance to the attempted overthrow of Aristide in 1991.

kongos   A term used in derogatory fashion for Haitian laborers.

Lafanmi Selavi   Literally, in Creole, the That's Life Family (as
  in *C'est la vie*), it could also be understood as meaning
  Family Is Life. Lafanmi Selavi is the name given to
  a shelter for homeless boys begun by Jean-Bertrand
  Aristide.

lambi   Creole for conch shell, used as a horn to call for the
  rising of slaves in the rebellion against the French colo-
  nialists, and since, for political rallying.

La Saline   Part of the city of Port-au-Prince, a crowded shanty-
  town partially built on landfill.

Lavalas   The Flood, and in the Vaudoun (Voodoo) religion, as
  in the Old Testament, a cleansing power.

loa   A spirit that, in the Vaudoun (Voodoo) religion, can possess
  a person, overcoming their individuality.

Macoute   *see* Tonton Macoute.

m'amie   Creole for my friend.

Manno Charlemagne   A popular Haitian singer whose song
  lyrics got people thinking about the possibilities of self-
  government. Independent minded and somewhat cyni-
  cal, he was nevertheless a vocal Aristide supporter. He
  was abducted after the coup against the elected Aristide
  government in September 1991.

merengue A dance, very popular in the Dominican Republic.

Misyon Alfa A literacy program taught through the Catholic church. Its reading series, called *Gout Sel*, or Taste Salt, was considered too radical by some of the church hierarchy (it used the word *dechoukaj* to teach the *D* sound), and the effort lost church funding in 1987.

Pe Creole for Father, and the usual way to address priests. Pe Titid is Father Aristide.

Petionville A wealthy section of Port-au-Prince.

Port-au-Prince The capital city of the Republic of Haiti.

Romain One-time mayor of Port-au-Prince, implicated in the contract selling of Haitian workers, often against their will, to the Dominican government sugar interests.

Ruelle Vaillant Street address of a school used as a polling place, where at least seventeen people were killed in November 1987 while waiting to vote.

sansmaman A Creole term for a good-for-nothing kid. Literally, without a mother.

taptap A car, van, or truck that picks up and drops off passengers on a more or less fixed route. *Taptaps* are usually very crowded, with passengers on the roof and sometimes clinging to the outside. When people want to get off, they tap on the roof or windshield.

ti soldat Creole for little soldier, the rank and file. A majority of *ti soldats* overthrew their officers in support of Aristide, in reaction to the attack on St. Jean Bosco Church.

ti kominote legliz Literally, in Creole, small church community. Called ecclesial base communities in other Latin American countries, these are the organizing cells of the poor as they put liberation theology into practice. Begun by the Catholic church, the hierarchy backed off as the base communities of poor gained voice and power.

tisane An infusion or tea.

Tonton Macoute   Literally, in Creole, an uncle with a sack on his back. In the old days this was an image used to frighten children, a boogeyman. The dictator François Duvalier organized a private army of thugs whose role was to terrorize any opposition. Deliberately sinister and anonymous, they took the name of *Tonton Macoutes*. Today *macoute* is a word used for bad guy, and *Macoutisme* refers to rule through terror.

zafra   A Spanish word for the sugarcane harvest, which can stretch from March through October.